Christina

SEQUEL TO *IN ITS TIME*

Nancy Rehkugler

authorHOUSE®

AuthorHouse™ LLC
1663 Liberty Drive
Bloomington, IN 47403
www.authorhouse.com
Phone: 1-800-839-8640

Published by AuthorHouse   04/16/2014

ISBN: 978-1-4969-0333-4 (sc)
ISBN: 978-1-4969-0334-1 (e)

Contents

Timeline of Characters and Significant Events, Dates and Locations from *In Its Time*

1902-1984   Dalton Duncan is born, dies in Seneca County at 82 years old.

1910-1984   Deborah White is born in Ithaca, New York and dies in Seneca County at 74 years old.

1918   Deborah's parents, Gordon and Susan White die in the Influenza outbreak, Debbie is 10 years old. She is taken in by her Aunt and Uncle. Aunt dies, left with uncle.

1928   Deborah White is admitted to Willard Asylum, mute, a rape victim, and pregnant.

1929   Deborah gives birth to a daughter, who is taken to the Foundling Hospital in NYC. Deborah was 19 years old at the time.

1929   Grace Shepherd Pope is adopted by John and Jeanette Shepherd of Greenville, Mississippi, via the Orphan Train. 1929 was the last year of the Orphan Train.

1947   Dalton Duncan is admitted to Willard, after World War II when he is 45.

1948	Deborah White and Dalton Duncan are released from Willard. They marry in 1949. Deborah is 39 years old. Dalton is 46.
1947	Grace Shepherd married William Pope. They have one child, Iris, born 1948.
1962	Elijah Marshall Fisher is born to Sebastian Fisher and Alberta.
1966	Iris Pope falls in love with visiting Italian Catholic teen named Dominico Crechea. That name is listed on the birth certificate, as the father.
1967	Delight Crechea Pope is born, child of Iris Pope and Dominico Crechea.
1967	Iris Pope dies following childbirth. Grace Shepherd Pope takes care of her granddaughter, Cressie.
1973	Grace Shepherd Pope dies in Indianola, Mississippi at 44 years old. Sandra Wright of Newark Valley, NY takes the child home to her sister, Ida and her husband Frank Williams. They adopt the five year old child, whom they name Delores Anne Williams, known as Del.

CHAPTER 1

DECEMBER 25, 2007

The dream wakes me in the early hours of Christmas morning. I don't know if I am more startled by the vividness of what I saw in my dream, or shocked by the sight of Eli in my bed. Then the events of the day before come flooding back into awareness. It had been a whirlwind year, filled with shocking revelations and surprising discoveries. I know more about who I am now, but more importantly, I am married to Eli.

All of the discoveries of the previous year led to our wedding on Christmas Eve. Last night, our wedding night, is the first time we have been intimate with one another. I can still feel the sweetness of it in my body, but even more in my heart. The sense of awe and wonder and mystery still lingers.

We will go today to see my father and the rest of my family in Newark Valley. They are expecting us for the family dinner. I called and warned them that I would be bringing Eli, a dear friend, though I did not elaborate on what that meant. I have mentioned him a number of times over the past few months, so at least it will not be the first time they had heard his name. I can only hope that they will not be disappointed that they were not present for our sudden nuptials. But our decision to have our wedding on Christmas Eve was literally accomplished overnight. We got the license on one day, waited the required time frame, and then stood before the judge friend of Eli's parents.

After that, Eli led the Christmas Eve worship service at his church. It all happened so suddenly that I did not even know where we would spend our wedding night. Eventually, we went to my house. Now I remember much of the evening, as my mind sheds its sleepiness. I also remember last night's candlelight service, and my hand shaking as I held the candle high during the singing of *Silent Night*. It was clearly a most holy night, in every way imaginable.

Eli's father Sebastian is in decline from his battle with Parkinson's disease. His mother Alberta is still in good health, but both are well into their eighties. We especially wanted them to be present for our wedding vows. Since Eli is an only child, he returned to the Syracuse area a few years ago to be closer to his parents during their advancing years. Eli is forty five years old, and I think, still in the prime of his life. After last night, it certainly feels that way to me.

I slip quietly out of bed not wanting to awaken my wonderful new husband of less than twenty four hours. I need some time to process all that has happened to me in the past year. On this day last year when I had Christmas dinner at our home in Newark Valley, my mother was still alive. Her death caused not only grief from loss, but also grief and confusion from the discoveries that followed.

There were the safety deposit box papers first, those mysterious documents, including a birth certificate, that hinted at another person's life, which I could not reconcile with my own. Over the past year, however, after all of the investigation, and connections revealed, I have begun to think of myself in a new way. Eli's friend Roger was the investigator, and he was giving us his final summary report when we discovered our own connection, so I suppose that I do not yet know the entire story of all that Roger discovered. I know that Roger was disappointed when we left so suddenly. I will have to read the summary report in great detail again. I am sure there is much yet to be revealed.

The amazing thing we discovered is that our love story seems to be the continuation of another love story which began with previous generations in both our families. The coincidences that brought us together are beyond mere happenstance, almost mystical.

Eli sleeps as I sip my hot coffee and ponder and remember. At forty years of age, I am a married woman for the first time. The reality is that Eli and I have actually spent very little time together, and probably do not know one another's particulars. I don't really know too many details about what kind of food he likes or doesn't like. Nor do I know what kind of toothpaste he uses. I don't know his taste in music or movies or books. I don't even know if the smell of coffee will wake him in the morning the way it does me. So far, he is sleeping.

Judge Worley, old friend of the Fishers, readily agreed to officiate at our Christmas Eve wedding, on very short notice. We scheduled a two o'clock time for the ceremony, and I arrived at 1:30. Eli's mother Alberta answered the door and gave me a warm hug. I could smell delicious food aromas coming from the kitchen. She told me that Eli was helping Sebastian get dressed for the occasion. The ceremony would take place in the library of their stately home. She let me peek inside before I was shuffled off to the library to wait until everyone was ready. She had filled the room, on every available surface with red and white poinsettias. There were also candles in two silver candelabras. I can only assume that those are family heirlooms. They stood on two small end tables set on either side of the fireplace. There was a lovely effect of the full flames in the fireplace, with the gentler flames of the candles flickering alongside. I could see that the intent was that we would stand in front of that fireplace to say our vows. It was a beautiful setting. I liked the symbolism of the flames, which in my mind represented the flames of passion, waiting to be consummated. Naturally, that was on my mind. I had waited a long time.

I had not been sitting and waiting for long when the door opens and Sebastian rolls his wheelchair into the room where I am. He reaches into his jacket pocket and draws out a small box, handing it to me.

"Del, I want you to know how proud I am for you to join our family. Nothing could bring me greater joy on this day than to be part of this wedding." He was dressed in a suit and a tie appropriate for the occasion. I knew it would have taken great effort for him to dress formally.

Sebastian opened the box and lifted from its slot a beautiful blue sapphire ring. It was the loveliest piece of jewelry I have ever seen, with diamonds on either side of the sapphire and tiny diamonds embedded in the band itself.

"I thought you might need 'something blue'," he said. "This is a family heirloom that belonged to my grandmother. So it also covers 'something old'. This ring has great sentimental value to me and I want you to have it. We always hoped that Eli would find a suitable wife, even though we could not envision what kind of person she might be. Berta and I both believe that you are the perfect match for our son. And thank God we are both able to witness this day."

I slid the ring on my right hand, and to my surprise, it was a perfect fit. Considering everything that has happened in our lives, I should not have been surprised. I could not hold back the tears. Sebastian was pleased by my emotional reaction.

I recall exactly how I felt at the time. It is three minutes before the hour of two o'clock, and I will soon enter the library and become a married women. In some ways, it seems natural; and it also seems completely unreal. I spend those last moments thinking about the people I have loved most. I remember my mother Ida and miss her terribly. I think about my father Frank and my Father, the Cardinal. I even think about my mother Iris and my grandmother Grace. They are all there with me, I know. Maybe most of all, it is my great-grandmother Deborah White who has brought me to this moment, reaching across the generations and the decades to touch my life, pulling me into her story. I thank God with all my heart for the people who have been my people, both through chance and through biology.

When I turn the corner and can see into the library, my heart pounds. Sebastian has rolled his wheelchair toward the right side of the fireplace, obviously taking his position. In front of him stood Eli, standing to the right of the flickering fire in the fireplace. Judge Worley stood to the side, gesturing for me to join Eli in front of the fire, and Alberta stood on the left side near the candles burning in one of the silver candelabras. It strikes me that when I take my position in front of the judge, we create a balanced scene, with Eli and me in the center facing the judge, and our witnesses Alberta and Sebastian are on either side. I can feel the warmth of the flames coming from the fireplace.

I look at Eli's beaming face. It is impossible to miss the joy shining there. Immediately, I feel a lump form in my throat, and swallow hard, trying to dislodge it, so that I would be able to speak. Although I cannot remember much of what the judge said, I do remember the essence of Eli's words to me.

"God has brought you to me, and I will honor you. God has chosen you, though neither of us knows yet exactly what that means. I have also chosen you to be my wife, and I do know exactly what that means to me. It means that I will always cherish you and encourage you and adore you. I will stand by you in sickness and in health, in disappointment and despair, in joy and in blessing. You are a blessing. I have never been more certain of anything in my entire life. And I also know that I will love you as long as we both shall live."

I cannot remember my exact words, but I do know that I gave my entire self, body and soul, to my marriage in those moments. I promised Eli that although I still have many uncertainties about myself, that I will lean on the strength of his certainty to sustain me. I will start with the power of his faith, and offer myself to God in whatever way I might be useful, if in fact, God has some special calling for me, or for us.

Also, I know that I promised to love and cherish Eli, and to honor him and be faithful to him, as long as we both shall live. I told him how grateful I am that he chose me to be his wife and how hard I will try to make sure he never regrets that choice. That room was filled with the power of the sacred swirling around and enveloping every one of us in its presence.

The sense of the spiritual was so palatable; it almost took my breath away. I have never experienced anything quite like it in my life, or at least, not that I consciously remember. Eli would say that I have had other significant experiences as a child. But as an adult, such matters are new to me, and still frightening. There is no fear in me now, though, in the presence of such overwhelming love.

+

It is Christmas day and I sit curled up in my blue floral chair, sipping on my second cup of coffee, deep in thought about the previous day's events. On my right hand is a beautiful blue sapphire ring given to me by Sebastian, a family heirloom. On my left ring finger is a simple gold band. I went from rarely wearing rings at all, to suddenly having one on each hand that I greatly cherish.

"Good morning, my lovely wife," Eli smiles from the bedroom door.

"Oh, hi Eli. Do you drink coffee first thing in the morning?" Because we have never spent the night together before, I do not know these things.

"Yes, ma'am. I surely do." He opens the cabinet and gets a mug and fills it with the hot brew. I have observed in the past months that he takes his coffee black. I, on the other hand, like mine with all the accessories. "Did you get enough sleep after our roller coaster day yesterday, and our passionate night?" Eli asks, grinning.

"Yes, it is a very merry Christmas indeed," I answer, though I can feel the color creeping up my neck. I have never had a husband before, especially following a night of lovemaking, and I feel somewhat flustered. Some of the previous evening replays in my mind and makes me blush. Then I remember the dream that woke me.

"I had a vivid dream, Eli."

"Anything you want to share?"

"If you won't laugh. I know that it will sound outrageous."

"Now you really have me curious."

"There was an angel of some sort. He did not have wings, and he looked like a man, but still, I knew he was an angel."

"An angel in your dream. And did this angel speak to you?" Eli asks.

"It wasn't like spoken words, really. I didn't exactly hear specific words. It was more like his thoughts went directly to my thoughts and I could pick them up."

Eli tilts his head to the side and runs his fingers through his hair with the hand not holding the cup. "Well, Del, as a biblical scholar, I can assure you that I would never completely disregard dreams or angels."

"And why is that?"

"Because there are too many accounts, especially around Christmas, where God speaks through angels."

"Yes, well, that's kind of scary, but I do wonder if that could be what was going on."

"What did the angel say?"

"First I got the message, and then a vision."

"Please do not keep me in suspense any longer."

"He said: *You are chosen.* I didn't say anything back to the angel, because somehow I felt that I wasn't supposed to be surprised."

"And then what?" Eli asks.

"And then I saw her," I answer.

"I thought the angel was male. Who did you see?"

"A little girl," I answer.

"Tell me the details."

"She was maybe about five or six years old, and standing in a meadow. She had dark brown hair blowing in the wind. It was a bright sunshiny day, and behind her was this golden light."

"Do you have any idea who she might be?" Eli asks.

"Yes, she is our daughter!"

Eli sits upright at this bit of information, and puts his mug down on the end table. "You saw a vision of our daughter?"

"Yes. Or, at least, I am as sure as I can be, considering that it was a dream. But that is clearly the message I got."

"Is there anything else that you know, or can tell me?" Eli asks.

"Nothing else that I can think of," I tell him. "But I know where she is."

"What do you mean, where she is?" Eli asks.

"She's in my womb, Eli."

"You mean now?"

"Yes, right now. She is beginning now. Don't ask me how I know. But I know with certainty."

"My God!"

Despite the certainty that I feel in my mind, it does not really seem at all possible, or for that matter, even likely. If fact, it sounds completely outrageous. I doubt that enough time has passed for a sperm to find its way to fertilize an egg, assuming there was even one there waiting.

But I can tell that Eli believes me.

CHAPTER 2

CHRISTMAS DAY

I tell Eli where to turn off of Route 38 just outside Newark Valley. It isn't far down Williams Road before our house comes into view. Eli lets out a whistle when he sees the Dairy of Distinction sign. The land that goes with our farm has been in the family for three generations. I tell Eli that on country roads, it is not at all unusual for the roads to be named after the land owners.

"Impressive," Eli says.

"Be sure and compliment my Dad. It would mean a lot to him."

"I'll try to remember. Tell me, Del, how shocked are they going to be when we spring the news on them?" Eli asks.

"I think they'll just be happy for us," I say, hoping that will be true.

I go over the names with Eli again. Frank Williams, father. Junior, older brother, and his wife, Linda. Their three children are Morgan, Francine, and the youngest Frieda. Morgan is twelve, the only boy. Francine known as Frannie, is nine, and Frieda, whom we call Freddie, is four years old. Even though I know you are not supposed to have favorites, Freddie is my favorite. She has unruly, red curly hair and a round rosy face. She is always animated and smiling, as if she is completely enamored with everything and everyone around her. She calls me Auntie Dee.

We pull into the driveway and Eli pulls up to the back door entrance, as I instructed. Dad is already there on the back porch with his arms spread wide. I jump out of my side of the car.

"Del, my dear, Merry Christmas," he says, giving me a big squeeze. Then he releases me and offers his outstretched hand to Eli. "Eli, welcome. We are honored to have you here today. For Del to bring you home on Christmas Day says a lot about how important you must be to her."

"You've got that right," I affirm, smiling.

"Auntie Dee, Auntie Dee," Freddie squeals, getting to me first, jumping up and down. Frannie and Morgan are not very far behind. They all give me big hugs. I notice that Morgan is getting tall. He is now taller than I am, by several inches.

As soon as we have the back door closed, Frank Junior appears and greets us warmly. "Merry Christmas, and welcome!"

I know that Linda is probably at the stove cooking. We are in the back mud room taking off our winter boots, and I am putting on our comfortable inside shoes. Thankfully, the temperature is just above freezing, with only a couple of inches accumulation of snow. At this time of year, the weather is completely unpredictable in upstate. For those of us who live here, Upstate is a separate entity, unique and distinct from downstate and the city of New York. The former is more rural and agricultural, the latter more urban and densely populated.

"Please come in," Dad invites.

The kitchen is filled with so many wonderful smells. I can tell there is an apple pie cooking, and probably a pot roast. Those two are standard for Christmas Day. I give Linda a big hug, and she greets Eli warmly, as we enter through the kitchen.

It does not take long before the meal is ready and all of us are seated at the table. I am surprised when Dad asks Eli if he will say grace for the meal. He does know that Eli is the pastor of a church. Even though saying grace is not something we always remember to do, I do think it is thoughtful of Dad to extend the invitation to Eli.

Then, before we actually begin eating, as the dishes are being passed around the table, and the noise level diminishes, it is Eli who breaks the news. We have not discussed exactly which one of us will tell them, or when. It seems to be something that Eli wants to get over with immediately.

"We have some good news to share with you today," Eli begins. "I hope this won't come as too much of a shock to all of you, but recently Del and I have realized just how much we love each other. I know that we have not known each other for very long, but we both believe it is long enough to be sure that we want to spend the rest of our lives together."

Every person stops what they are doing, and puts down their utensils, as if to ponder that, and to listen carefully. Clearly, they are shocked.

Dad says, "Well, that is good news. I guess we should welcome you to the family, Eli. I am assuming that kind of a statement includes an intention to marry. Is this an engagement?"

Eli begins, "Actually, we got married yesterday."

There is a long pause of silence, and then he adds, "I do apologize that you all were not at the wedding, but it was a very sudden decision. And we do hope that you will all give us your blessing."

It is Linda who speaks first, breaking the ice. "Del, that is so great! I am really happy for you both. Let's start passing this food around while it is hot, and you two can fill us in on everything that has happened."

Everyone does seem to be genuinely happy for us. I am relieved.

Dad says, "We do give you both our blessing. And welcome to the family, Eli."

We tell them about Eli's work, about his parents and Sebastian's illness. Then the conversation turns toward matters of faith.

"Well, Eli, I'm sorry to say that we haven't been regular church folks. We are more the Easter and Christmas kind," my Dad says somewhat apologetically.

"I understand," Eli says, "and please do not feel like you own me any apologies. I am grateful to have

Del as my wife and my partner. Del will participate in my ministry to the extent that she is comfortable doing so. I don't have any particular expectations of her and won't be pressuring her to fill some spousal role."

"Do you know where you will live?" Junior asks.

We look at each other. I answer this time. "We actually have not worked out the details yet. Eli's parents have a very large house, and Eli has been helping with his father's care. I suspect that we will spend some of our time there."

Then Eli adds, "But we will not move Del's things out of her home, at least not any time soon. I think it might prove very beneficial for us to have our own space, a retreat house."

I am pleased to hear that Eli feels that way, although we have really never discussed the specifics of our permanent living arrangements. It is a bit shocking to consider all of the things we have not yet discussed.

As the dinner progresses, the conversation turns to farming, and Eli does remember to ask Dad about the Dairy of Distinction, which gives my father the opportunity to share his convictions about that recognition and to brag a little about our farm.

"I understand that you have two hundred and fifty milking cows," Eli says. "Do you grow your own feed?"

Soon Junior and Eli are deep in conversation about the most efficient farming techniques. I cannot believe that Eli knows so much, and specifically knows what questions to ask to engage both Junior and Dad in lively conversation.

Junior recounts how two weeks earlier there had been an ice storm. The entire farm lost power, but in the milking parlor the backup generator had kicked in. Dad told about the time there was an outbreak of a mastitis infection. Eli asked how they delivered the milk to market, and Dad filled him in about the pipeline that runs to the tank, and how Dairylea comes regularly to pump out the tank. Junior talked about his future plans to produce biogas from manure. Linda even joined in the conversation, telling Eli how this year has been an especially good year for the price of milk. The profit margin for the dairy promises to be significant for 2007. That is most certainly not always the case. Linda says happily that it will be a good year for her to go for a shopping day at the Binghamton Mall after Christmas.

Eli and Dad find common ground in the discovery that both of them had been Eagle Scouts. They compare notes on their experiences, and talk about the merit badges they had each acquired. Eli's most memorable experience is his Emergency Preparedness Merit Badge. My Dad excelled in First Aid. He recalls the many times over the course of his life when he has actually used many of the things he had learned. I am surprised to learn that my Dad still takes First Aid courses whenever they are offered to the community by the Fire Department.

I learn for the first time about my father's Eagle Scout Project, which had been the construction of the gazebo in the village square in the town of Newark Valley. He had to appear before the City Council and submit plans and a budget, and get permission for the project. He also recruited other builders to help with the project. That is the way he spent the summer after he graduated from high school.

I learn that for his Eagle Scout project, Eli cleared and constructed a trail at Green Lake State Park. The construction part involved several sets of stairs, as the hill was steep in parts and needed to be more accessible. It also involved cutting back tree roots to make a level walking path.

Later when I ask Eli about his knowledge of farming, he smiles and says that he always likes to be prepared and had done his homework. I am already very impressed with my husband, but after this, I believe him to be absolutely brilliant! He credited Google with his brilliance.

I help Linda with the dishes. Morgan and Frannie clear the table. After the dishes are finished, we head for the Christmas gifts, which in our family is limited to the children. Long ago, we abandoned any expectation that the adults would get gifts for one another and decided that Christmas gifts are supposed to be for the kids. The children have already opened their gifts from their parents. Now they are excited to open the ones I have brought. They squeal with delight at each one. I do spend time trying to find a really special gift for each child.

After the gift opening activity, Dad takes Eli on a tour of the farm. I stay behind with Linda and the kids.

I wonder what Eli's conversation with my Dad might include. Later on the way home, I did ask.

"Eli, what did you and my Dad talk about?"

"I assured him it wasn't a shotgun wedding."

I laugh. It did not occur to me that he might have thought that, considering the speed with which we got married. But then it occurs to me—the time might come in the months ahead when he will wonder about that, at least if my dream turns out to be true.

Eli and I hold hands on the drive home, and share all our thoughts and feelings about the afternoon. It has been a really lovely visit and Eli can see how fortunate I am to have been adopted by such a family. And all of them, without exception, were quite impressed with Eli. They did not even have to say it out loud. I could see it in their eyes and demeanor, all the way down to four year old Freddie, with whom he had played some hide and seek after dinner. I could see from his interaction with the children that Eli will make a wonderful father.

Just being able to discuss the experiences of the day and of the evening is something new in my life. I have lived a solitary existence most of the time without anyone to talk to and share my day's events. How good it is to be able to share with someone who cares and listens.

We return to my house early in the evening, which is now our house, or at least one of them. I could never in my wildest dreams have imagined the depth of both passion and tenderness that I experienced on that Christmas night. We are only beginning to discover one another and our needs and responses and desires. It is a delicious experience.

I have never really dared to imagine what it could be like to be married to the man you love. It is glorious.

Chapter 3

January 12, 2008

Eli and I have settled into a pattern since the new year began. We spend weekdays at his parents' home in Chittenango. It is a very large house with seven bedrooms and at least six thousand square feet. We staked out an area for ourselves upstairs, at the opposite end of the house from where Alberta and Sebastian sleep on the first floor. As newlyweds, we do not want to feel inhibited, and our corner is far enough away that we can be confident that we are not heard in our private moments. Alberta brings in extra help to stay overnight over the weekends, and we stay at my cottage.

I still do feel more relaxed and at home when we stay at my carriage house. Our upstairs living area at the Fishers does not have a kitchen, so at our 'retreat home' we can go directly from bed to the coffee pot without worrying about being seen by others, and without the need to get dressed. Now that I think about that, perhaps we could just put a coffee pot in our upstairs Chittenango bedroom.

++

I have been back to work now at Golden and Golden law firm for almost two weeks, and I cannot believe how much I have changed! I once loved my work as a paralegal and took great pride in it and always wanted to excel. Now my mind wanders. And it wanders into the most unexpected places. One minute I am thinking about sex. The next minute, I am wondering about theology, or thinking about Eli's sermon on Sunday. Now I am curious about those things, though just three months ago, I was not.

There is quite a mix of heady material rolling around in my brain these days. My scope of interests has definitely broadened. One thing I know that I want to do is to read a book of theology. How amazing that I would get to that point in my life! I want to understand what Eli does and how he thinks. I want to understand grandmother Grace and how she came to her unusual ministry, especially in her time and place. There are more women preachers these days, but they are still not in the majority. She must have been such an anomaly, especially in Mississippi in the 1970's.

I suppose I would have to read the history of the Catholic Church to gain insight into the inner workings of Cardinal Conti, my biological father, and how he came to his place in the church. Surely, not very many people are able to claim a Cardinal as their father, given the Catholic expectation of celibacy. Since women are not allowed into the priesthood, I also wonder what the Cardinal would think of my grandmother Grace Shepherd and her preaching.

It has only been less than a month since I heard the summary of all the investigation into my past. Roger Riley did that work, Eli's long-time friend. Last year was filled with constant turmoil, beginning with my mother's death in January and ending with my marriage in December. In between those two major life events, I learned that Frank and Ida Williams adopted me, more or less. I discovered that I have other biological parents and ancestors. My mother Iris died in childbirth at nineteen. It was my grandmother Grace who raised me. Since that revelation, I have recovered some memories from those early years of my childhood.

I remember what it was like to hear my grandmother preaching. As my grandmother and caregiver, she could not have been more gentle and kind. But as a speaker who preached before a group of worshippers, she was transformed into a powerhouse, almost unrecognizable to me. Even as a young child, I remember vividly listening and watching her intently, as everyone else was. She was such a gentle soul, and such an unlikely person to take on that kind of power.

Actually, this journey of discovering that I have a different past from the one I have always known started when I visited the Willard exhibit at the Everson Museum. Although I had no idea at the time, the familiar looking picture that I saw there that day was my great-grandmother Deborah White, mother of Grace Shepherd Pope, who raised me during my early years. My story is almost unbelievable. I do recognize that I am a different person now, since discovering my past. Eli helped me to accept my past and to embrace it. We talk about it often.

The truth is, I am still making connections between myself, Delores Williams, now Delores Fisher since marrying Eli, and my great-grandmother Deborah White who spent twenty years at Willard, a Psychiatric Hospital in upstate New York. I recognized right away that we have the same initials. But beyond that, I have also recognized how many other similarities we share in our stories.

I have re-read the Summary Report provided by Roger Riley about my family and my past. Roger still calls me every few weeks to check in and see how things are going. There is still unfinished business associated with all of the information he provided, which hopefully I can someday piece together and understand completely. For one thing, I would like to drive to Willard, New York and see what is left of that campus, even though it now is dedicated to other uses. Roger tells me that I must someday see the memorial in Indianola, Mississippi, built in my grandmother's honor. That is obviously something that impressed him and moved him.

I can trace my story back to Gordon and Susan White of Ithaca. They both died of the terrible flu epidemic of 1918. Deborah would have been eight years old at the time. They all appear in the census of 1910, the year she was born. Deborah next appears in the records at Willard when she was eighteen years old. I will probably never know all that happened to her, but I do know that she gave birth while she was there, and the baby was put up for adoption. That baby was my grandmother Grace.

My grandmother Grace had a photograph of Deborah White, which had been tucked into her baby blankets when she was delivered to the Shepherds on the Orphan Train. It was the same picture that I saw in the safe deposit box following my mother's death, and then again later at the Everson Museum exhibit about patients at Willard.

In some ways, the story of my life is a sad story, but I prefer to think about it in a more positive way. Later in her life, Deborah White was happily married to her husband Dalton Duncan. She became an artist of some renown, at least in central New York. Deborah's daughter Grace became a powerful preacher who made a difference in this world. She raised me early in my life, at least until her tragic death. It is my hope that I may also make some positive contribution to this world someday, though at this moment I do not know exactly what that contribution might be.

Deborah lost her mother to a terrible flu epidemic. I lost my mother at childbirth. As a young child of eight, Deborah witnessed her mother's death from influenza. As a child of six, I witnessed my grandmother's murder. When Deborah lost both of her parents, she was all alone in the world with no one to turn to. I actually do not know the details of how she ended up where she did, at Willard. I may never know. When my grandmother was killed, I had no one left. It was a friend of my grandmother who brought me to her sister in upstate New York, the Williams of Newark Valley.

I have learned that my great grandmother Deborah did not speak for a long time, perhaps years, during her institutionalization at Willard. My mother told me that I did not speak the first year I spent with them on the farm. Both of us—Deborah White and me, Delores Williams, were dealing with incredible loss and grief. And both of us ended up happy later in life. I like to think that my story is more a happy story than a sad one.

I have realized all of these things only recently. Everything that I have discovered about my past, and everything that has happened to me during this past year, does make me wonder about the future and what it might hold. Already, I have learned so much, changed so much. What more could possibly happen?

Chapter 4

Christina

It is Saturday morning. I know that Eli always goes in to the church and spends some time there before he preaches on Sundays. I know that he practices his sermon out loud, and I know that he also spends some time in private prayer. There is a part of my husband that will always be a stranger to me. I cannot claim the faith he has, or the same kind of relationship with God he enjoys. It amazes me that he has never been bothered by my lack of church experience or religious knowledge. Incredibly, he does not expect nor demand that I have the same level of faith or understanding. I wonder whether or not he might even prefer being married to someone who is quite different from him.

Usually, I am the early riser in our family, though for some reason, Eli got up early this morning. As I fix my cup of coffee, I can feel his eyes on me.

"Eli, you are staring," I chuckle, not feeling particularly stare-worthy in my silk pajamas, with mussed up hair.

"I am licensed," he says.

"Licensed?"

"Yes, licensed to look and to enjoy and to please."

"Ah, the marriage license. Well, yes, thank heavens for that. And you do please me in every way, Eli."

"I adore you my Delight Pope Delores Anne Williams Fisher."

Before being Delores Williams, at birth I was originally Delight Crechea Pope, love child of Iris and Nico. That is my other story. I am adjusting to it, getting used to it, claiming it.

"Well, I don't get called all of those names very often."

Eli then stands and embraces me and kisses me with every ounce of his masculinity and power, which are considerable. As usual, he takes my breath away.

"You are glowing this morning, my dear," he says.

At that comment, I think that I should share with him what I am thinking.

"Eli, I have something I want to tell you." A slight look of anxiety flickers across his face. He steps back and looks at me closely.

"I do think I am late with my period." I know because as a rule you can set your calendar by my periods. Mine should have started around ten days ago.

"Well, you did warn me, so I cannot say that I am surprised."

I see him stop momentarily. I know he has something else he wants to say, so I wait until he speaks.

"And her name shall be called Christina," Eli says with a serious look on his face.

"What makes you say that, Eli?" I wonder, somewhat shocked by the strangeness in his voice, and the way he phrased that. It sounds like some kind of a proclamation.

"I heard it in a dream," he adds.

"Are you serious?"

"Yes, totally, just last night. That's why I am up early this morning. It was a very vivid dream and so striking that I could not go back to sleep afterward."

"What exactly happened?" I ask.

"Well, I did not really see an angel in my dream, but I knew that I was visited by one. She simply said to me in a very clear voice—*and her name shall be Christina.*"

"So what do you make of all of that, Eli?"

"I take it to mean that you were right. I assume that you got pregnant on Christmas Eve, our wedding night. I assume we will have a little girl, and that we will name her Christina."

"Wow! Now we both had a dream. That is a little scary."

"Are you okay, Del?" Eli wonders. I assume he is asking how I am handling all the strange events that always seem to be happening in our lives.

"Yes, I am fine. But I must admit that between my dream and your dream all of this is rather eerie," I add.

"I probably would not choose that exact word. But I will have to admit that unusual phenomena of one kind or another have been with us ever since we met."

"You mean, like that time I found myself pulling off the road and into the parking lot of your church, as if someone else had taken over the steering wheel." I have never really understood how I ended up inside that church for the first time.

"You never described it to me like that before," Eli comments.

"Maybe not. I already feel strange enough, without bringing up something else far out."

"Should you go and see a doctor, Del?" Eli asks all of a sudden, presumably wondering about a possible pregnancy.

I chuckle. "I might just try a pregnancy test first. I'll get one this morning while you are at the church."

"Will you wait until I get home before you actually take the test, and look at the results?"

"Of course, if you wish."

+

When Eli got home in the afternoon, I took the pregnancy test, and just as we suspected, it turned up positive. Still, having that actually confirmed was a monumental moment for us, and we laughed and embraced and celebrated.

Eli told me later about the sermon he had already prepared for tomorrow. On the liturgical calendar, the lesson for the next day is about the baptism of Jesus. Eli preaches the lectionary, those scriptures that are selected for and attached to each Sunday of the calendar year. He also often ties the sermons and the scripture selections to the things that are going on in his own life, as if he is personally living the liturgical calendar.

Eli reminds me of the story from Advent of Elizabeth and Zechariah, and how an angel told Zechariah that his wife would be with child. Zechariah did not believe it, since they were so old. The angel was not pleased with Zechariah's unbelief and he was struck dumb until after the child was born.

He sees our own story as having a connection to Elizabeth and Zechariah, not only because of their advanced age and ours, but also because of their son John's connection to Jesus, whose birth we celebrated at Christmas. Our own child was conceived that same night.

The son of Elizabeth and Zechariah was John the Baptist, the prophet who told of the coming of the Messiah, and the one who would baptize Jesus in the Jordan. Today we confirmed the existence of our child in the waters of my womb.

Eli explains to me that it was quite shocking for him to have that dream about the name of our daughter, and to be preaching about John the Baptist, and learning of my pregnancy all at the same time.

Now that I have become more curious about this sort of thing, I later actually go and pick up a bible to see if I can find the section about John the Baptist baptizing Jesus. It does not take me long to locate it. It seems to me that there is more information about these events in the Gospel of Luke, so I read there.

I read the words: *And the Holy Spirit descended upon him in bodily form like a dove. And a voice came from heaven. "For you are my Son, the Beloved; with you I am well pleased."*

I immediately remember my experience as a child when I felt a bird fluttering around me. I was about five years old at the time and my grandmother Grace was preaching. The bird seemed so real to me. It fluttered around me for what seemed like a long time. I even cried out, "Bird, Bird."

Eli tells me that there are places in the bible where the Holy Spirit is described as a dove. He even suggests that my bird experience was probably an experience of God's spirit, coming near, touching me. To this day, I am mystified by that idea.

Maybe Eli would not choose the word *eerie*, but I do find our coincidences eerie! I have a dream and believe that an angel tells me I am pregnant. Then Eli has a dream and is told the child's name. I just don't know what to make of all of that.

Maybe the best thing for me to do is to just not think about any of this for a while. I can just read a good book. In that particular moment, the one closest at hand is the Gospel of Luke, so I read that, from the birth of John the Baptist, to the ascension of Jesus. I had never read the entire story before. I must admit it is quite fascinating.

Maybe most of all, I am surprised at how much interaction Jesus had with women. I thought that in the patriarchal society of biblical times, women had no place. Jesus does not seem to operate that way. I am amazed.

CHAPTER 5

MARCH 1, 2008

I am making toast for myself in the kitchen at the Fisher house, as I have come to call it. I am a Fisher now, so I suppose that means that it is my house too. I am more and more at home here, as each day goes by. Alberta appreciates my presence, though I am not a great deal of help. She just enjoys the company, I think. Sebastian's illness has caused him to go downhill so much in the past couple of months.

A year ago, his Parkinson's only presented with symptoms of tremors, mostly on one side of his body. By the end of last year, he was much less steady on his feet, and out of fear of him falling, Eli and Alberta got a wheelchair and insisted that he use it. His mind is still sharp, despite his physical limitations.

At this point, all of Sebastian's physical abilities have diminished. Talking and swallowing have become more difficult, though he is making a valiant effort at both. Sebastian is a man of great accomplishments, and equally great pride. I can see that Eli has a lot of his father's pride, both in his physical posture, as well as in his approach to life. A proud man like Sebastian makes high demands on himself, and then by extension, those around him. Sebastian's speech is now soft and monotonous, though not yet slurred, and he sleeps many times during the day.

Eli and I decided to wait until I am three months pregnant before we tell his parents. I so badly want to tell them, but realize that it is much better to wait to reduce any likelihood of disappointment. I am considered a high risk pregnancy, with a first time pregnancy at age forty. But the truth is, I have never felt healthier. I have suffered no morning sickness, and Eli swears that I am aglow. I certainly feel that inside. So far the pregnancy has been very easy.

I will admit that I am constantly wondering about the matter of my own calling, if indeed there is such a thing. Eli thinks that the scene which happened to me when grandmother Grace died, may have something to do with me and my future. As a young child, I believed I heard her speak to me, as she departed this life. The spirit said, "You are Elisha." Now that I remember that event, it weighs heavily on my mind. If I am to pick up her mantle, so to speak, I have no idea how that might unfold, or even if it ever will.

++

Eli went to Princeton Theological Seminary and graduated at the top of his class. I often wonder how a person like that could ever have been attracted to a person like me. There was a brief period of time when I thought about seminary, but now that I am pregnant, that is not something I plan to pursue. I did ask Eli one night exactly what the process is for preparing for the ministry. The truth is, that process, or those processes, are all attached to one's membership in a particular church, or denomination or tradition. And they differ, depending upon the denomination to which one is affiliated.

I am an anomaly, not having grown up in any particular church, not really affiliated with a denomination. And now my husband is the pastor of the Community church I attend in Jamesville. Eli explained to me that the path toward ordination is a long one. I have a two year degree with a specialty in being a paralegal. But a bachelor's degree would be required before being a full time seminary student. I did a search on the internet and found that there is a seminary in Rochester—Colgate Rochester Crozer Divinity School. Rochester is within commuting distance for me. The list of the courses is quite fascinating. One does not have to be an admitted student just to take a course. The truth is, I dream about doing just that. I haven't told Eli about my interest in the divinity school, but when the time is right, I will. My plan is to just take one course, and see how that goes. There is no timeline in my mind, just a desire. Historically, Colgate Rochester is affiliated with the Baptist Church, but its students come from all persuasions. Maybe I will not stand out as being as unusual as I feel.

By the time Eli was nineteen, he was attending a Presbyterian Church. He got his church start in an evangelical church as a youth, but ended up attending the First Presbyterian Church United in downtown Syracuse, one of the oldest Presbyterian churches in Syracuse. He told me that he had became curious about that church because that is where Sebastian and Alberta had their wedding. They both knew so many people at the time, they needed a large sanctuary to accommodate the gathering.

Alberta told me a fascinating story about their wedding. Sebastian was always a generous person, and he never hesitated to give money to the homeless people he encountered on the street. He was known far and wide among the homeless for his boundless generosity. In fact, on the day of their wedding, Alberta said that a group of about thirty of the street people showed up outside the church. One of the deacons came and asked Sebastian what he wanted to do. He wanted to invite them in. And so they did.

Eventually Eli's ordination took place at the First Presbyterian Church United in downtown Syracuse. At its heyday in the 1960's, the church had over one thousand members. These days the congregation is down to about two hundred and fifty members. Eli was twenty five years old when he was ordained there. I wish I could have seen that. Alberta tells me it was quite the grand occasion.

Alberta comes into the kitchen while I am drinking my coffee. I did put a small coffee pot on our bathroom counter upstairs, but it is just not the same as the coffee maker in the kitchen, which makes coffee of exceptional quality.

"Good morning, Del. You are looking quite lovely these days. Marriage must agree with you," Alberta comments.

"Hi, Alberta. Needless to say, marrying Eli is the best thing that has ever happened to me. How is Sebastian these days?" I ask.

"He manages to keep his spirits up most of the time. Depression is a common side effect of this disease. At least he is not crushed by that, at least not yet. But his blood pressure has been really low lately."

"You're doing a great job, Alberta. I know he really appreciates you."

"Thanks, Del. Oh, how I wish you could have seen Sebastian when he was younger. He was such a powerhouse of a man."

That comment makes me think of Eli. I have often wished that I had been part of his earlier life, and some of his major life events, like his ordination. But I know those are jealous thoughts, wanting more than I have at the moment. I try not to wish for what I cannot have, or might have missed.

Although I can see a great deal of Sebastian in Eli, I would not have used the word *powerhouse* to describe Eli. That certainly does apply when he preaches, but in general, Eli is an unassuming man, completely unaware of his good looks and his charm and the effect he has on others. I find Eli to be highly intuitive, which is a different kind of power.

Eli says that as a lawyer his father was a great orator. I can say the same thing about Eli as a preacher, though he would never think that about himself. He is always modest.

"Oh, by the way, Del, before I forget, you had a call yesterday just before you got home. It was Roger Riley," Alberta says.

"From Roger? I wonder what he wants," I comment.

"I wondered the same thing, and in fact, I asked him."

"What did he say?"

"He said he has a recent discovery to tell you about," Alberta says.

"Well, that sounds intriguing. I'll give him a call today," I promise.

"I offered to give you a message, but Roger said this was something he has to tell you in person."

"Oh."

Any occasion of seeing Roger Riley always feels to me like taking a ride on a roller coaster. Roger is someone who loves to live by speed and danger. His friendship with Eli seems so very unlikely to me.

I smile to myself, realizing that Eli shows a pattern of being attracted to people who are not at all like him.

And I do thank God for that!

CHAPTER 6

ROGER'S NEWS

I meet Roger at Starbucks in Fayetteville. He was five minutes late and made an entrance, flirting with the barista. I already had my cappuccino Venti, French vanilla. I rarely frequent Starbucks, but I always have found it impressive how they have managed to create a particular culture with its own language. It is more like having an experience, than a cup of coffee.

Roger kisses me on the top of my head before he sits down.

"What's going on?" I ask immediately.

"No foreplay at all, huh?" he teases.

"Okay. Hello Roger. It's good to see you. You are looking good these days. What discovery do you have for me?"

"Del, you just aren't going to believe this!" Roger says.

"Try me," I prod, intensely curious. Roger has often been a bearer of shocking news in my life.

"Well, how closely did you read the Summary Report I gave you?" he asks.

"I read it all the way through two times," I answer. It was hundreds of pages long. I certainly did not remember every detail.

"Do you remember my interviewing Carolyn Wilson in Seneca County?"

"Not anything specific, really."

"Well, here's a quick summary. Carolyn Wilson used to be Carolyn Oliver, daughter of Harold Oliver, good friend of Dalton Duncan."

I do recognize the name Dalton Duncan. He was the kind man who had married my great grandmother Deborah White. And as we later discovered, he was also a long lost relative of Eli's. In a strange way, it was their connection that sealed the deal for us. We see ourselves as being a continuation of their love story, several generations down the road.

"When I finished interviewing Carolyn in Ovid last year, before I left I gave her my business card. I said that if she ever heard anything else about Dalton or Deborah Duncan, to let me know. I didn't really expect to hear from her, but I always leave my card, because you just never know."

Roger takes a swig of his coffee, and pauses, looking around at the other customers. I am getting annoyed because I want him to get to the point.

"Well, it turns out that Carolyn's husband is a real estate agent in town. He was selling a house there in Ovid. It was an old house, so the people who were buying the house insisted that the seller put in new insulation in the attic. The insulation guy came across this thick notebook, which he gave to Carolyn's husband Jack. Jack brought it home for Carolyn to read. She could not believe her good fortune. The book found in the attic turned out to be a personal journal written by none other than Deborah While. Apparently that was a house that Dalton and Deborah once lived in in Ovid."

"You mean, you have a journal written by Deborah White herself?" I marvel. I have a moment of hope that I might learn more about her.

"Well, some of it, and knowing her story like I do, I think it is amazing that suddenly she has a voice and we can hear her speak."

"That is unbelievable! Are you going to give it to me?"

"I can only give you what Carolyn Wilson gave me. It turns out that our friend Carolyn wants to keep the journal for herself. Finders keepers, and all that. My guess is that she is probably thinking about publishing it," Roger adds.

"Can she do that?" I ask.

"Of course, if she can find a publisher," Roger says.

"Do you think she will?" I wonder.

"Honestly, that would not surprise me. As you know, it is a very compelling story."

"How much of the journal did she give you?" I ask.

"She gave me copies of about thirty pages. She selected what she thought you might most want to read," Roger says.

"Well, it doesn't seem right for her to be the one to decide that. I would be interested in all of it."

"I understand, but I doubt that you would have any legal claim to the journal."

"I suppose not. Where are the pages?"

"In the car. I'll give them to you when we leave. But first, fill me in on Eli and what's been happening with you guys."

I fill him in as best I can. It is hard for me to keep our pregnancy a secret, but so far, I have. I talk about Eli and how things are going at church, and how intrigued I have become with religious matters. Roger does not appear to be particularly interested in that. I tell Roger about Sebastian and Alberta. He has known them all of his life, since he grew up with Eli. Roger is sad to hear about Sebastian's illness progressing.

"And you, Roger?" I ask.

"What about me?"

"Exactly," I respond. "What have you been up to?"

"Top secret spy stuff," he grins.

"I'll bet," I grin back.

CHAPTER 7

DIARY

Deborah White is my great-grandmother. My own story traces back to her parents, Gordon and Susan White of Ithaca, New York. Both her parents died in the influenza outbreak in 1918 when Deborah was eight years old. I have always assumed that I would never find out what happened to her during those missing ten years.

Deborah White ended up at Willard Asylum when she was eighteen years old, and it was later discovered that she was pregnant. I have often thought about that, and how young she was. Did she even understand what was happening to her? In Deborah's journal, she writes about how she felt about giving birth. In the pages that I have, she does not mention the rape. She also wrote about her years at Willard, about meeting Dalton Duncan, and how they were fortunate to be released into the community. She and Dalton Duncan were obviously happy together. Deborah gained some fame as a local artist around Central New York.

I learned from her journal that she was tormented for much of her life by the child who had been taken away.

This is some of her story in her own words.

From Deborah Duncan's Diary　　　　*November 15, 1951*

Considering the life I have previously lived, I have been really quite happy after Dalton and I married. He has always been so good to me, so tender and loving and devoted. Our marriage is even better than I ever could have imagined. We have built a good life for ourselves. Dalton works at the Army Depot and I devote my time and energy to my art.

Of course, I have always known that I still have inside me a lot of pain, and baggage, and unresolved issues. For a long time, I met with Dr. Taylor in Trumansburg. She is a wonderful therapist and has been very instrumental in my healing and in helping me to let go of my past.

The one part of my past that I have never been able to leave behind is the agony I feel over the loss of the little girl to whom I gave birth. I wasn't much more than a little girl myself, even though by then I was institutionalized at Willard. I figured that I must be pregnant, since my periods had stopped, but I was in denial, and for a long time after the rape, I did not speak.

I did scream and cry out during labor. That much I remember vividly. I could not believe that those sounds were escaping out of the mouth of this silent self. I was frightened by the sounds of those screams.

Wounded and afraid, I understood that I could not care for a baby. I could not even care for myself. But I felt her life and her presence when that baby was growing inside of me. I even began to feel a sense of attachment, even though I never thought that would happen. That surprised me. And after a while, I intentionally stopped remembering the way she had been conceived. That was not her fault. I could not hate her for that. If my own circumstances had been different, I could have loved her. I do love her.

I have always felt comfortable talking about my feelings about the baby to Dalton. He fell in love with me despite everything that happened to me. I know he understands. So often he has shaken his head sadly, and said how he wishes our lives had been different, that we could have met earlier. He has confided in me how much he wishes that we could have had a child of our own. But of course that was not to be.

The only child I ever had is the one born at Willard, and taken away. They did let me hold her for a while before she was taken away forever. I think I must have had about half an hour with my baby. She was so beautiful. I could not believe she had come from me.

I had no experience with prayer, but I know that is what I spent all that time doing, begging God, if there is one, to bless this child. Please dear God, bless this child. Give her a good and loving family. Help her to grow up well. Bless her in all the ways I cannot even imagine. Protect her from harm. Make her a blessing to others. Give her good people to love. Don't let the kind of things that happened to me, happen to her.

I turned my heart and soul inside out, screaming inside and pleading for mercy for this infant. Over the years, I have come to believe that whatever God there is, heard this mother's pleas that day and answered those prayers. I have a sense of peace about that.

Still, there is a sadness in my soul, an emptiness, a hole. Somewhere there is a young woman to whom I gave birth. And I will never know her. She would be twenty eight years old now. I try to picture her as a grown woman.

I was able to learn, several years after leaving Willard, that my baby was sent to the Foundling Hospital in New York City. Infants from there were adopted out all over the country, but so far, I have not been able to learn where my little girl went.

Most of the Willard staff knew us or knew of us. Dalton and I were unique, as far as residents go. We got out. We got married. We lived to tell our story. And we do not live very far away. Dalton goes back and talks to people over and over again, and asks them questions, to see if there is anything at all he can find out, or if anyone remembers. Someone suggested that he might be able to find Nurse Hazel, who had been there at Willard the longest. She left Willard long ago, and Dalton learned that she also left the area.

Her name sounded familiar to Dalton. It triggered a memory that he had, from years before. I could not believe that he had never remembered this before. But suddenly, Dalton remembered talking to Nurse Hazel when he first came to Willard, wanting to know about me. It turns out that she vividly remembered when I had the baby. That was not something that happened every day there. Hearing Nurse Hazel's name brought that conversation back to Dalton's memory.

Nurse Hazel told Dalton that she had taken a photograph of me from the file and tucked it inside the blankets of the baby, right before the baby was taken away. Hazel told Dalton that she hoped that picture might someday mean something to someone.

It's not much, I know. Not much real information. Not much to go on. It is nothing at all that would help me to find her. I can only hope that that picture is out there somewhere, and might someday lead her to me. That is my hope. That is my prayer.

It's not much, but you just never know.

~~

I cried so hard I could not see to read any more. That snapshot had gone with the baby to the Foundling Hospital, and had also accompanied her when she was sent out for adoption. There had been those who understood how important it might someday be to that child to have a picture of her mother.

When I piece all of that together in my mind—the photograph and its role in my life—I have an idea flash into my brain, and I know with absolute clarity exactly what I have to do. And I know that I want to do it fairly soon. It is the least I can do.

Hopefully, Eli will be able to go with me.

CHAPTER 8

A PLAN

Eli likes to take Fridays off. He has all his Sunday preparations done by then, and is better able to relax and have a day of rest. We stay later in bed on Fridays for that reason. I can always anticipate early morning cuddling and its inevitable consummation, which never grows old. We feel we need to make the best of the time we have left before the pregnancy gets seriously in the way, which we assume that it will. Then after the birth, the baby's needs will inevitably take precedence over ours.

"Well, good morning, my love," Eli smiles at me. I roll on to my side facing him.

"Hi, honey."

"I can tell that there has been something on your mind for a couple of days."

"Well, yes, but I cannot believe you know that."

"I can read your face, your posture, the little line between your brows. Why don't you just tell me what it is, and let's look at it together," he suggests.

"That's probably a good idea," I sigh, amazed at my husband's keen sense of observation.

"I'm guessing that it has to do with the journal Roger delivered to you," he speculates.

"Yes."

"So what did you discover?"

"It isn't so much a new discovery, as it is a new idea."

"Spill it, Del. My curiosity is getting the best of me."

I told Eli then about Deborah White discovering that a nurse had put a photograph of her, the mother, with her baby who was being put up for adoption. He recognizes instantly that it would have been the photograph that I discovered first in my mother's lockbox papers, and then later in the Everson Museum exhibit. The old photograph had first been transported from Willard to Greenville, Mississippi where the newborn girl had been adopted. Years later, it was transported to Newark Valley, New York, along with a little girl named Cressie.

I was called Cressie in my early years when I was being raised by my Grandmother Grace, as I have come to call her. The nickname is a shortened version of Crechea. Grandmother Grace must have treasured that photograph of her biological mother, because it was in the "important paper" envelope that Aunt Sandy brought with her, when she transported me to Frank and Ida Williams, my adoptive parents.

The photograph ties the generations all together. It is a photo of Deborah White, who gave birth to a daughter she never knew. It is a photograph that Grace's adoptive parents eventually gave to her when she was old enough to understand her own origins. It is a photograph that found its way into my possession when my adoptive mother Ida died. And then from there, my world shattered and the year of investigation began.

And now I am pregnant. It may well be because I am pregnant that I want to bring this story somehow full circle. I want to return to my Grandmother Grace the photograph of her mother, whose name she never knew. I want the grieving mother Deborah White to finally be reunited with her lost daughter. I want to tie all of us together somehow—my own mother Iris Pope, my grandmother Grace Shepherd Pope, my great-grandmother Deborah White, and myself.

"I want to go to Indianola, Mississippi and I am hoping that you will be able to come with me."

"That's where your Grandmother Grace died."

"Yes."

"When do you have in mind going there?"

"Soon."

"Can it wait until after Easter? I will have a couple of weeks off after Easter, and we can plan a trip then."

"That will be fine, Eli. I was hoping that I would not have to go alone. Or with Roger."

"No way!"

"Are you jealous of Roger?"

"I actually trust Roger not to violate our friendship. And I certainly trust you as my wife. But I know he would flirt and enjoy that. I'd just rather not give him that pleasure. I'll take that pleasure for myself. And I do think it would be an interesting trip. What exactly do you have in mind?"

"Well, I have talked with a memorial plaque company out on Erie Boulevard and they can turn an old photograph into a tombstone plaque. They can laser engrave a photo of your loved one onto a black granite plaque. You simply attach the engraving to a headstone. They use a special high strength outdoor tape that secures the memorial plaque to the headstone. And it comes with clear instructions."

"I'm impressed, Del. You have a plan already."

"Yes, in fact, I have already taken my photograph to the engraving company and ordered two different plaques."

"Why two?"

"I want to put one on the grave of my Grandmother Grace, probably somewhere on or around the memorial monument. The other one I want to put on my biological mother's grave. Iris Pope. The research shows that she is buried in the Indianola City Cemetery. Grace lived there in Indianola when Iris died. I have written different words for each one, but all our names will appear on the plaques, from Deborah's to mine."

"You've given this a lot of thought," Eli comments.

"I think this may be related to my own pregnancy. It is all somehow connected, the pregnancies, the births."

"I'm not sure just why, but somehow this reminds me of the story of Ruth."

"Well, it would, Eli. You always connect me to that story for some reason. I've never really understood why."

"You're right. It's probably because I was preaching about Ruth and Naomi when I was first keenly aware of your presence."

"And what did you think?"

"I thought I wanted to see more, to know more."

"And so you do. Now you've seen it all."

"Actually, I believe that I have only just begun to scratch the surface of all there is to know about this very intriguing person who is my wife. And then there are our children. God knows what the future might bring!"

"Children? Plural?"

"Why not?"

"I'm not so young, Eli," I protest.

"Sure you are."

Suddenly Eli pushes me back down on the pillow and places his hands on my stomach. I am not really far enough along for there to be much of a bump there. But the pregnancy is very obvious in my breasts, swollen now and tender. He kisses my belly first, and then each breast.

As always, he takes my breath away.

CHAPTER 9

EASTER

It has been quite a few years since I went to Easter services with my parents in Newark Valley. The Easter celebration this morning is wonderful. Eli has always said that he loves Easter, and now I can see that passion lived out in worship, and in his sermon.

I especially love the sanctuary filled with all the Easter flowers and spring flowers of every kind, at least every kind that grows from a bulb. It is the bulb that makes it an Easter flower, I have come to understand. The bulb is the tomb out of which the beautiful new thing grows, like the resurrection. Like the womb.

Of course, in a public setting, there are always people who are allergic to flowers, and that becomes a problem. Whose need should prevail? Those who want to enjoy the flowers, or those who are allergic? At Eli's church, Jamesville Community Church, they came up with a most creative solution to that. About twenty five years ago, the way the story goes, a woman named Fran Morris went to see the pastor about her Easter flower allergies, which were severe. They made her eyes and nose water, and caused constant sneezing. When she complained to the pastor about that, he simply asked her what she would suggest. And thankfully, Fran Morris had already given that some thought. The church typically had an early morning service in the Chapel, a smaller service, but important to those who attended. Fran suggested that the Chapel service become the flower free service.

"How can we make it festive, without the flowers?" the pastor asked.

"Well, Pastor, I have two large ferns at home that I'd be happy to bring in. They're big and lush and fancy," Fran offered.

"I like that idea," he commented.

And thus was born what came to be known as The Fern Service. Practically everyone who came to the early service, as well as the allergic folks who normally went to the later service began to bring a fern to dress up the chapel. It was a sight to behold. In fact, the volume of ferns in the early service sometimes even surpassed the volume of Easter flowers at the later service. In both cases, every available surface, including the floor was filled with either flowers or ferns. Eli said he thought it had turned into a competition. In his mind, that was a good thing, because it got more people interested and involved than ordinarily would have been.

In fact, the local florist has learned to special order ferns for Easter, as well as lilies, though many people just nurture their ferns at home and bring them back each year, decorated with large white bows. Eventually, parts of the story merge together and most people now think it was Fern Morris who started The Fern Service. At this point not many people even remember that her real name was Fran. I heard the story from one of the older ladies who was much younger at the time, but still remembers how it all got started.

I have never really given a lot of thought to the meaning of the resurrection, at least theologically. I am only now just beginning to think theologically. Once we got past Good Friday, I could see a lighter, more hopeful, cheerful, upbeat Eli emerge. I observe that he holds back his natural joy during Lent. That is a strange thought, giving up joy for Lent, but that's what I'd say Eli has done, at least in his worship leadership. Thankfully, he does not bring his liturgical mode home. At least, it may still be there all the time, but he does not lead with it at home. At home, he is the loving and attentive husband, not the pastor at all. I will confess that sometimes when he is the pastor in the pulpit, I blush thinking of our bedroom activity. I have to censor my thoughts on those occasions.

Eli said that the resurrection is all about second chances, and I can relate to that. It is all about a new day, a new beginning, and I have lived that personally this past year. I am a new person indeed. I have to admit that I am even getting to the point, over time, where I think I can say that I am a new person in Christ. I gather that is all about being set free from your burdens of guilt or sin or shame or whatever drags you down or holds you back. I know that I am in the middle of that process, and sometimes wonder where I might end up.

The few people who have heard my story probably wonder about that also. My grandmother Grace was shot to death inside the church where she preached. It was on a Saturday. I was a five year old little girl Cressie. I witnessed that terrible scene and was traumatized into silence for a long time afterward. The adult Delores, who now knows the whole story, or at least much of it, remembers the feeling that my grandmother's spirit came to where I was hiding under the pew and spoke to me. She had been preaching about Elijah the prophet passing along the mantel to Elisha.

What I thought I heard was my grandmother saying '*You are Elisha.*' I certainly did not know what that meant. And truthfully, I still don't. I am familiar with the biblical story now, that Elisha picked up the cloak that Elijah, the prophet, left behind. I have no idea if I understood the voice, or whether or not those were actually the words I heard. It is all a mystery to me. I have no idea what I am supposed to pick up or do or become, if anything at all. And honestly, I am in no rush to find out.

My life is about as full and exciting as I can handle right now. I have just enjoyed a wonderful, beautiful Easter. I am expecting a child. When we get back from our trip, I will be at the three month mark, and Eli and I agree that we can share our wonderful news. I cannot wait to tell my family, and to tell Eli's family. I know that this pregnancy will be both a surprise and a delight. The odds of a first pregnancy at forty years of age are slim, and they begin to diminish significantly after that. We are blessed, in every conceivable way. Literally.

I am so glad that Eli and I are making this trip together to Indianola, Mississippi. I especially want to see the monument built in honor of my grandmother Grace Shepherd Pope. Even though I have seen pictures of it, it is difficult for me to envision.

I have communicated with the Chamber of Commerce in Indianola and I have assured them that I am Grace Pope's closest relative. I told them about the plaque that I want to attach to Grandmother Grace's monument. They graciously agreed, but they did request that I visit their office first to show them what I have prepared. All communications with that office have been gracious and cordial. I look forward to meeting them.

I have discovered that my biological mother, Iris Pope, is buried in the Indianola City Cemetery. I have also prepared a plaque to add to her headstone. I am assuming that hers is much smaller than my grandmother's monument. The plaque I had made is also smaller. That one was also much more challenging for me to sign my name, all of them, both of them, the original, the current ones. Iris's memorial plaque has an engraved photograph of me, as I look today. I am hoping that I may be able to find a photograph of

Iris as she was around the time that I was born, just to satisfy my curiosity.

I made all the trip arrangements. Eli was completely occupied with Easter events and preparations. Next year, I plan to be more involved at church than I have been this year. First, I just need to go through a year's cycle, and pick and choose where I might best fit in at the church. The people there are quite welcoming, and most do seem thrilled that Eli has married. I have no doubt that there are a few broken hearts, women wishing it had been them.

One thing I am beginning to see is that regardless of what ministries I might pursue, some people will always see me as my role, that of pastor's wife. I plan to resist the expectations that go with that. The truth is, I'd rather be myself, than be identified simply as a wifely helpmate. I am beginning to understand what some of Eli's concerns might have been.

Making the trip arrangements included flight plans, hotel reservations, and reserving a car. We are flying into Memphis, and driving to Indianola from there. It should be an interesting trip.

Chapter 10

March 24, 2008
Indianola, Mississippi

We learn that the car rental places are just off of Democrat Road, and not on the airport premises. We catch the bus to the Hertz lot, and pick up our car, a Toyota Corolla. After studying the map, Eli determines that Interstate Route 69 will take us over to Rt. 61 South, which we want to travel from Memphis to Indianola. Almost immediately after we start driving on Rt. 61, the terrain is very flat. Soon I notice that a mirage precedes us along the way. At first I do not know exactly what it is. It looks amazingly like rain on the road.

"The mirage is an optical illusion," Eli says.

"What causes it?" I ask, figuring that Eli will know the answer.

"It's an optical illusion caused by a thin layer of hot air just above the ground. The difference between the hot air on the surface and the cooler air above makes the road act like a mirror," Eli explains. The mirage is actually a reflection of the sky.

Many of the towns and streams and counties have Indian names. Arkabutla. Coahoma. Choctaw. Mound Bayou. Besides the flatness of the land, I am struck by the color of the land next to the road, the shoulder of the road, and the color of the road itself. Everything has a reddish brown tinge to it. We stop along the highway a couple of times, once for coffee, another time for a bathroom break. The sound of the spoken language is often difficult to understand. There is an extreme twang-like drawl along with unfamiliar pronunciations. I can only pick out a few words. The further into the delta we travel, we notice that the population appears to be predominantly African American.

Two of the larger towns along the way are Clarksdale and Tunica. Clarksdale has signs for a Delta Blues Museum. Tunica has a thriving Casino economy, at least along the highway. Most of the towns themselves are not directly on that highway. Perhaps that is what gives it such a desolate feel. There are long stretches of nothingness. We encounter little traffic. As we drive along the highway, passing many small towns along the way, the one consistent sight is a school-bus-yellow rectangular Dollar General sign. The Dollar General stores are all located along the highway, rather than in the downtown part of the town itself.

We drive past several small rivers. They are also a brown and muddy color, perhaps best described as the color of coffee with cream. I recall that the Mississippi

River itself is sometimes referred to as the Big Muddy. Although we have not actually seen the Mississippi River, I know that it is to our west, as we travel south.

I notice that already spring flowers are very much in blossom, some even past their prime. The daffodils must have bloomed weeks ago, since they are looking droopy. Trees with white blossoms are in bloom along the road. I do not know the name of those, but they are lovely. All the trees have at least some visible signs of green leaves, some fully blossomed. There is still snow on the ground back home in Syracuse. Here, spring is well under way.

It is about a two and a half hour drive from Memphis to Indianola. On the outskirts of Indianola there is a huge Dollar General warehouse with hundreds and hundreds of trucks lined up endlessly. That warehouse is large enough to supply all the Dollar General stores for half the state.

We arrive in Indianola around three o'clock in the afternoon. I have booked a room at the Best Western on Rt. 82 and we go to check in. The clerk at the desk says, "Are you familiar with Delta water?"

"Not really," I answer, though when I went to the bathroom at a service station, I had noticed that the water is brown.

"The water has a brownish color to it, and that comes from the cypress tree roots. It is safe but we do give our guests bottled water," she says, putting two large bottles on the counter for us to take.

Since it is only mid-afternoon, I think that we might have enough time to locate the Chamber of

Commerce and find Steve Haley, a member of the City Council with whom I have been in communication. I have been instructed to meet him there. He is going to look at, and presumably approve the memorial plaque I have brought for my grandmother's monument.

The front door is open to the brick building on Main Street. A receptionist greets us warmly. Her thick southern drawl has a delightfully slow and sweet sound to it, signaling that life here is lived at a different pace.

+

"May I help you?" she asks, smiling.

"Yes, I am Del Fisher. I have been communicating with Steve Haley about a memorial plaque. Is he here by chance?"

"Oh, yes he is, Mrs. Fisher. He is expecting you, though we thought it might be tomorrow before you got here," she says.

"This is my husband Eli Fisher."

"Mr. Fisher, welcome to Indianola."

"Thank you."

"Let me go and get Steve for you." She hurries off to an office down the hall. Eli and I smile at each other. She does seem excited that we are here, though I cannot imagine why.

Soon Steve Haley greets us and directs us to his office, gesturing to the two chairs across from his desk. He appears to be around fifty years old.

"Well, I'm mighty happy to meet ya'll," he began, in the drawl I am growing to enjoy and appreciate. The sound of it reminds me of my grandmother.

"Let me just share with you right away that I took the liberty of contactin' some folks I know who attend the New Pentecostal Church here in Indianola," Haley says.

"Oh," I comment, puzzled.

"Yes, ma'am. When I mentioned to a couple of folks about ya'll coming, of course there are still some folks around who knew your grandmother Grace. Her husband Will Pope was also something of a legend, a real decent man, and an educator here in the Delta, God rest his soul. Your grandmother we just refer to now as Angel Grace."

"Because of the monument?" I ask. Eli is letting me do all of the talking, at least for now, which I appreciated. This is my pilgrimage and he is my companion.

"Well, yes ma'am, and probably some other things too." I assume he is talking about the years of her ministry in this town.

"Word got out at the Pentecostal Church about your visit and there is one woman there in particular who is just real excited to meet you. Her name is Aida Sinclair. She told me that you used to sit with her during the services, back when Angel Grace was preaching at her church."

"That's absolutely amazing," I say. I could not believe that a person's imprint could still be felt and known after forty years.

"She's seventy five years old now, but still as sharp as a tack. She wanted me to give you her phone number and address and tell you that she sure hopes ya'll will stop by to see her while you're here," Haley says. I take the piece of paper.

"It's actually not very far from here, and real easy to find, just one turn off of Rt. 82."

"Thank you very much, Mr. Haley. I'll be sure to give her a call. Tomorrow we'll be going out to the monument site and I have the plaque here that I want to attach," I mention.

I reach into my large gray purse and bring it out. It is wrapped in tissue paper and then placed inside a manila envelope. I take it out of the envelope and carefully remove the tissue, handing the plaque to Steve Haley. He reads it and smiles and nods, returning it to me.

"That's mighty nice, Mrs. Fisher. I don't know the whole story, but I do know from what you have told me that you are trying to draw together all your ancestors. I do admire that."

"This is something I really need to do, so I appreciate your cooperation," I say. I have certainly been impressed with how cordial everyone has been.

"The site is well maintained. There was enough money in the memorial funds donated to make sure that the place is well kept, out of respect for Mrs. Pope, our Angel Grace. As I am sure you have noticed, we don't advertise that site in our tourist brochures. I'm sure you can understand why. What happened to her is still an embarrassment to my fair city, even all these years later," Steve Haley says. "It's not something we would like to be known for."

"Of course. It was a terrible tragedy," I add. I am not especially inclined to tell him anything about my own memories of that occasion. Those are still new and fresh, having only been recovered several months ago. That was a big part of my journey of self-discovery last year, recovering some memories. Learning the truth of my story had been a lot for me to deal with. My biological mother died shortly after my birth. My grandmother, who raised me, was shot in her own church. My great grandmother was institutionalized in a psychiatric hospital. The truth is that is a terrifying past for me to try to absorb. I am making progress.

The best part of that journey of self-discovery for me is that in the end, it led me to Elijah Fisher, to whom I am now married. That makes all of the anguish and uncertainty I went through well worth the effort.

We are about to leave Steve Haley's office. He seems a little restless, like he is not quite ready for us to go out the door.

"Uh, there's just one more thing. I probably shouldn't say anything, but there are rumors about the place."

"What kind of rumors?" Eli asks.

"Well, it's hard to say, really. Different folks have had different rumors. Some people report strange things happening."

"Such as?" I ask, a little taken back.

"Wind blowing there, when it isn't blowing anywhere else." Haley says.

"I see," I respond. But of course, I don't really.

"One or two folks swear they were healed out there," he adds.

"Healed physically?" Eli asks, curious.

"More spiritually, I think," Haley answers, though it is clear he does not want to give any details. He does not appear to be entirely comfortable with the conversation.

"Hmm." we say together, puzzled.

"Just thought you folks ought to know."

CHAPTER 11

IRIS

We take our time entering into the day, eating a leisurely breakfast. The Best Western offers a full breakfast buffet with selections for any taste, from the biscuit and gravy lovers, to the cereal crowd, to the yogurt and fresh fruit options. Eli prefers some kind of a sweet roll, while I enjoy toast with my coffee. He thumbs through the *The Enterprise*, a local newspaper of Sunflower County, while I look at the USA Today, a complimentary copy.

Eli and I decide that we will first go and visit Aida Sinclair in the morning, have lunch at the Catfish Cafe, and then visit the angel monument in the afternoon. We call Aida and she is thrilled to hear from us, just as Steve Haley predicted. Her place is indeed easy to find. It is one turn off the highway, a small brick house with badly overgrown shrubbery around the front. My first thought is that maybe she doesn't have anybody to trim it for her, and she would not be able to do that herself, at seventy five years old.

Aida meets us at the door. She is rather stoop shouldered, with a bun of white hair twisted into a knot at the nap of her neck.

"Well, ya'll come in, come in! I'm so happy to see you. So you must be little Cressie all grown up?" she clucks. *You* sounds more like *yew* when she says the word.

"This is my husband, Eli, Mrs. Sinclair."

"Aw, honey, you can just call me Aida if you want to."

"Thank you Aida. And thank you for seeing us," I say.

"Mrs. Sinclair . . . Aida, we heard from Mr. Haley that you knew Del's grandmother, Cressie's grandmother," Eli says.

"I did indeed. I did indeed. Would you folks like some iced tea. I already made it first thing this morning. Let me go and get it. I hope ya'll like sweet tea," she says.

"Yes, thank you," I answer.

Eli and I both look around the room which is filled with family photographs, both in frames on every surface, and covering the walls as well. Aida sees us looking at them when she comes back in the room with the tray.

"I have four great-grandchildren," she says proudly.

"Really? That's wonderful," I comment.

"And how many children do you have?" Eli asks.

"I have five children, fifteen grandchildren, and four great-grandchildren so far."

"How fortunate you are," I remark.

"So do you have a family," she asks.

"Not yet," Eli answers.

"We've only been married since Christmas. We got a late start," I add. "You know, I'd love to hear about my grandmother."

"Do you remember your grandmother Grace?" Aida asks.

"Only in little bits and pieces," I confess.

"You know, Cressie, you left kind of sudden like. Those of us around here never really heard the whole story of what happened to you."

My mind whirls, trying to find a succinct way of telling her my story. I do not have the energy to tell it all. But I try for a quick summary.

"My grandmother had a friend named Sandra Wright who lived across the street from her. Apparently Grace had some inkling that something might happen to her, so she asked Sandra to take care of me, if anything did happen. Sandra took me to Upstate New York, to her sister and brother-in-law. They adopted me. I became Delores Williams. I was traumatized by witnessing my grandmother's death, and did not speak for a long time. Also, I repressed all the memories of my early childhood and didn't even remember being Cressie Pope. When my adoptive mother died last year, I found my adoption papers and put the pieces together. I also began to remember some things about my grandmother.

"Like what sorts of things?" Aida asks.

"You'd think I would remember the personal things, the times at home, her taking care of me, but really, many of my memories are from church. I remember her voice and what it sounded like when she was preaching."

"Yeah, that's hard to forget," Aida says.

"Was she that great a preacher?" I ask.

"I suppose, but it wasn't so much her skill at preaching as it was her power. She had power and authority, if ya know what I mean."

"I think I do, Aida. My husband Eli is also a preacher, and I've experienced that same kind of thing in him."

"Well, goodness me, married a preacher, huh?" She nods at Eli with appreciation. "Miss Cressie, is there anything in particular you would like to know?"

"Were you close to Grace? Were you friends?" I ask.

"I'm not sure you'd say I was her personal friend. There was something special about Grace that made her feel real spiritual and extraordinary. And kind of remote. I do know that she trusted me. She asked me one time if I would sit with you in church while she was preaching. You were a quiet child, most of the time, at least, and no trouble at all. I think mostly she just didn't want you to feel lonely." Aida let out a chuckle all of a sudden.

"There was that one time when I couldn't get you to shush up. You disrupted everyone. It was not like you."

"Tell me about that," I ask.

"You thought you were seeing birds inside the sanctuary." My heart skips a beat, hearing this. Eli looks at me and his eyes grow large. I know exactly what he is thinking.

"Mrs. Sinclair. Could you tell me if you saw anything?" Eli asks.

"Not really. I can't say I saw anything, but I did hear something."

"What did you hear?" we both ask at the same time. But we both already know what she is going to say. This is something I have remembered and wondered about. Eli has speculated on its meaning.

"Wings," she says. "I heard the sounds of fluttering wings."

"What did you think it was, Aida?" Eli asks.

"Well, after thinking about it all these years, I'm wondering if it maybe wasn't some angels flying around."

I ask her if she had ever discussed that incident with Grace.

"I did. In fact, I went to see her the next day to ask her about it. To tell you the truth, I was kind a taken back by her answer," Aida says.

"What did she say," I ask.

"She said it was just the Holy Spirit swirling around you, Cressie. I expected her to be happy about that, but I could tell that it made her uncomfortable. Why do you suppose that would be?"

Eli tries to answer that one. "Maybe she was worried that God wanted her grandchild for God's own purposes."

"And wouldn't that be a good thing?" Aida asks.

"Well, maybe not always." Eli answers truthfully. After all, it had not ended well for Grace Pope.

++

Aida soon brings out some sugar cookies to go with our iced tea. The tea is ten times sweeter than I am expecting, and it is challenging to drink. This must be the southern version. Eli and I are still trying to take in what we have learned so far. I am completely unprepared for her next comment.

"I knew your mother Iris," she says.

"Oh, my goodness, you did?"

"Yes, she was a beauty. She finished up her high school years at the Indianola Academy. Every boy in town would have loved to date her, but she never showed any interest in a single one of them. In fact, one of my own boys, Johnny, was sweet on her for a while. Then she went off to The W. That's where she fell for the Italian fella. Oh, that reminds me, I don't want to forget! I've got something for you."

Aida gets up off of the couch with some effort, and scuffles ran off to a bedroom down the hall. I explain to Eli that The W is a shortened version of Mississippi University for Women in Columbus. It is the oldest state supported women's college in the country. Soon Aida is back, holding a piece of paper close to her chest.

"Steve Haley knows that Johnny used to be sweet on Iris. That's why he contacted me to tell me ya'll was coming to town. I remembered that my boy Johnny had tucked Iris's picture away in his high school yearbook. I thought you might want it," Aida offers.

My hands go to my chest. I am afraid that my heart will jump right out of it. I look over at Eli, who just shakes his head in disbelief. Here is another picture from the past, mysteriously re-appearing after many years, to tie us all together. I have never seen a picture of my mother Iris. Aida hands me the picture. I look at it and immediately start crying. I do not even try to hide my tears. Here in my hands is a picture of my biological mother Iris Pope. She was truly beautiful. There is something deeply moving about seeing her for the first time. I can see that I do not especially resemble her. But I already know that I look more like my biological father, Cardinal Conti.

We thank Aida profusely. I never expected to find such a gift as the picture of Iris, which I will always treasure. Once again, a surprise photograph comes unexpectedly into my life.

Because we are going to stop by and see Iris's headstone first, before going to Grace's memorial monument, I ask Aida where we might find some flowers. She gives us directions to Indianola Floral Designs on Main Street, which is not very far away. She tells us it is run by Amy, a home town girl. I understand that is important to Aida.

While we are there, I buy two large bundles. After all, I do not expect to be down this way again anytime soon, or perhaps ever.

+++

We drive down Sunflower Street which takes us to Main. There at the end of the street is the new BB King Museum. There is a new part of the Museum, attached to what had once been a cotton gin where King had once worked. A left turn takes us along the bayou. I am amazed by the trees growing right up out of the water. We stop to take pictures. There is also some kind of moss hanging from the trees, though it is not Spanish moss. There is green algae standing on top of some of the bayou water. Soon we come upon the entrance to the Indianola City Cemetery.

I want to add the memorial plate I had prepared for Iris's headstone, but I do not know exactly where it is located. We wander around for quite a while before we find it. The headstone has her name and the dates of her birth and death, with words beneath:

Iris Marie Pope
1948-1967
Beloved Child

There is plenty of room beneath the engraved name to attach the plaque I have brought, which reads:

To my biological mother

Iris Pope
From your daughter
Delight Crechea Pope
and
Delores Ann Williams Fisher
One and the same.
Born April 6, 1967

++

When I am finished placing the flowers, I happen to glance at the headstone just past Iris's. Much to my shock, I discover that Grace Shepherd Pope is actually buried here at the Indianola Cemetery, next to her daughter. Just beyond her is her husband William Pope. I am surprised by this discovery. Somehow, I thought that my grandmother's Memorial site was also her burial site, but that turns out not to be true. I wonder why Steve Haley did not told me, but I realize that I never mentioned to him in our communication about my intent to visit Iris's burial site.

But of course, it makes sense for Grace to be buried here in the cemetery, next to her husband and next to her daughter. I also remember that it had taken time to decide on what her memorial would be like and where it would be located.

At first, I wonder about what I should do with the plaque I have prepared for Grandmother Grace's Angel Memorial. I conclude that it is a little too large to affix to her headstone in the cemetery. In the end, I decide the right thing to do is to take the plaque to the Angel Memorial, as arranged with the City Council.

But I do pause for a moment and feel deeply moved to realize that here we all are—my grandmother, my mother, myself, and my unborn child. Four generations. I want to mark the moment in my mind and hold it dear. We are women who might never have known one another's stories. Nevertheless, we are bound together through the ages.

As much as it was possible to do so, this moment brings us full circle.

Chapter 12

Grace

Steve Haley has given us detailed directions to the monument. The next morning we travel east on Pollack Road for a couple of miles. The large stand of trees on the right, just past an abandoned cotton gin on the left signals our turn-off. I have no specific recollection of the utter flatness of the Mississippi delta. As a young child, I was too young to notice that detail. It would have been just normal to me back then.

On the open road, you can see for miles. It is a beautiful sunny warm day, with temperatures into the high sixties, although rain showers are predicted. I cannot help but notice that the highway in the distance is always filled with a mirage, slick and mirror like. We encounter another unexpected weather phenomena on our way to the memorial. There is a rain shower up ahead. We can actually see it. It has a clearly defined beginning point into which we drive, like driving through a curtain into the raining area. A few miles down the road, we drive through the curtain out of the rainy area. It is the strangest thing, not at all like a rainy day in New York.

We do find our way to the designated place. I have seen pictures of the monument which Roger Riley had taken. He had been especially enamored of this particular place, which was unexpected to me. Roger, Eli's best friend, and an investigator, is a worldly guy. He does sometimes surprise me with the things that move him. Once in a while, I wonder whether or not he has more heart than he lets on. I suspect there is a tender spot in there somewhere, which he keeps tightly under wraps.

We drive half a mile down the curved Dogwood Lane, and then the clearing in the midst the trees comes into view, and there it is. Not only is the monument amazing, but the surrounding trees are in full bloom, bright pink dogwood. When I see the name of the Lane, I do remember seeing those beautiful trees before, as a child. I know there is something else about the dogwood trees that I cannot quite remember. Maybe it will come to me.

"That's spectacular," Eli is the first to speak.

"I can see why Roger was so impressed," I add. We both look at the angel statue.

"He is so happy that we are making this trip. I can't wait to tell him all about it. I'll take lots of pictures, too," Eli says.

As soon as I open the car door on my side, I feel a gentle breeze that I have not noticed before. It seems to be swirling mostly around me, but I do not make any comment about that. I am sure that I am imagining it, having been spooked by Mr. Haley's remarks.

An angel constructed from broken pieces of brick and steel rods and cables and wires does not sound enchanting, but enchanting is the best possible word to describe it. The base itself, upon which the angel stands, is about four feet off the ground. The square base is approximately five feet in width on each side. The angel herself is maybe another ten feet high above the base. I cannot tell exactly. The monument is impressive both in its size and in its quality. It is a most unique artistic rendering, created from the remains of a leveled church. I have never seen anything like it before.

On one face of the base there is a plaque crediting the artist who constructed it. I know that Henry Gill worked on it for years and years, but died before its opening and dedication, though it was already complete. That much I do remember reading in Roger's report.

Another larger marker is attached on the northern side of the base, memorializing Grace Shepherd Pope, 1929-1973. I quickly decide that I will attach my own memorial marker on the south face of the base. Removing the cleaning kit from my purse, I begin to clean the section where I will attach my plaque. I was assured by the monument company that if I follow the directions exactly, the memorial plaque will be securely attached for many years to come. When the area is clean and prepared and dry, Eli holds the level, getting the bubble dead center, so that the plate will be perfectly straight. I do not want it to be askew. I press it in place, and stand back to look at it.

In loving memory of my grandmother,
Grace Shepherd Pope,
Daughter of Deborah Lee White Duncan
1910-1984
(The engraved photograph of Deborah White is in the center.)
Given by
Cressie Delores Pope Williams Fisher,
Daughter of Iris Pope
1948-1967
(Engraved photograph of Del Fisher, 2008)

May God bless the generations past
and the ones yet to come.
In this place we come full circle,
We are one.

As soon as I stand, I can feel the wind grow stronger around me.

"Eli, do you feel the wind?"

"Del, I don't feel it on me, but I can see that it is swirling around you, blowing your hair and your clothes around." Eli has a stunned look on his face, not exactly sure what to think or do.

"I think I would like to have just a few minutes alone to speak to my grandmother, Eli."

"I don't want to leave you."

"Then just walk a little way down the lane, back toward the road."

"Okay, but I'm not letting you out of my sight," Eli says reluctantly. I can tell he is unnerved.

I can feel something happening around me, and inside me. It is not at all frightening. If anything, I feel uplifted. I feel a cool sweet breeze on my face, a caress, and suddenly I am compelled to kneel with one hand on the memorial plaque I have just attached to the monument. I kneel on one knee and pray, as unfamiliar as this pose is to me, as unexpected as the urge.

I thank them all, my ancestors, and think of all they had been through. Deborah White wept over her newborn little girl, whom she had never forgotten. Grace Shepherd gave birth to one daughter, Iris, who gave birth to me. Grace then lost her only daughter, and I my mother. So much loss. So much pain.

Yet none of that is what I feel in these moments. I feel an overwhelming sense of love and hope and joy. I pray for the child within me, that she might somehow be spared the pain and loss my ancestors have known. I pray like I have never prayed before. I am so moved spiritually that tears are streaming down my face.

I feel raindrops hitting my skin. That is unexpected, out of the order of things, considering the sunny day we have been enjoying. I look up at the sky. Before I know it, Eli is by my side.

"Something is going on, Del," he says.

"I know."

"What is it?" Eli wants to know. Surprisingly, I know the answer.

"A blessing."

No sooner have I said that, than the rain lightens, and a rainbow stretches across the sky, directly above us. Light is all around. I soak it all in. It fills every fiber of my being. I feel warm and alive and utterly at peace.

For some reason, I remember reading about the legend of the dogwood tree. At the time of the crucifixion, the dogwood had been the size of the oak and other forest trees. It was strong and firm and chosen for the cross and its cruel purpose of crucifying Jesus. After that, never again did the dogwood grow large enough to be used for a cross. The blossoms form the shape of the cross. In the center of the outer edge of each petal there are nail prints, brown with rust and stained with red. In the center of the flower there is a crown of thorns and all who see it will remember.

++

CHAPTER 13

MAKING CONNECTIONS

As we drove back to Memphis to get our flight home, Eli and I talked endlessly about all we had seen and experienced on our journey. I had accomplished so much more than I ever could have dreamed. I never dreamed that I would end up with a photograph of Iris, or meet someone who had actually known her. I suppose I should not be surprised. In the past couple of years of my life, even stranger things have happened.

Eli held my hand as the plane descended at the Syracuse airport. The trip home had been a long day. We returned the rental car, caught the shuttle to the airport from the car rental location, and gritted our way through a long layover in Charlotte. The pilot said that there are clear skies in Syracuse, and we are descending. I was definitely ready for a good night's sleep. Before we turned in for the night, Eli wanted to know how I was.

"Del, how are you feeling?"

"You mean, besides being tired."

"I mean about the pilgrimage. Is it all you hoped for?"

"Yes, honey, somehow it was very helpful to my spirit. I feel as if I have tied up a lot of loose ends, knitted something together that was somehow frazzled, but is now perfectly in order, complete."

As soon as I described it that way, I will admit that even to me, that does sound a little bit like healing. I had not recognized it as such at the time. But maybe that is what happened back there. Maybe Steve Haley was right about that.

All the broken and misplaced pieces of myself seem to have fallen into place somehow.

++++

Eli comments that morning, "You seem different, Del."

"How do you mean?" I ask.

"More lighthearted, more relaxed."

"Well, of course, it has been more than three months now, and so I can share my pregnancy news. You know, I've been thinking about a middle name for our baby."

"A middle name," Eli repeats, cocking his head to one side. I can tell that he has not given that much thought, which surprises me. I know already that her name will be Christina, at least according to Eli's dream. But she still needs a middle name. Most of the generations in Eli's family have had middle names of Supreme Court justices. Eli is named after Justice

Marshall, the justice who served the longest with thirty four years. Sebastian is named after McKinley. He never could figure out why they chose him, a man from Alabama. Sebastian found some consolation in the fact that at least his namesake was a Democrat. His grandfather Fisher's name was Oliver Wendell Fisher. Wendell had served for thirty years. After him, it had become a middle name trend that ran in the family.

"Did you have something specific in mind?" Eli asks.

"Yes, *Ruth*."

"You mean, as in Ruth and Naomi?"

It never occurs to me that Eli would think of that. "Well, no, as in Bader Ginsburg."

Eli shook his head in either amazement or amusement. I am not sure which one. "You know, my dear wife, you never cease to amaze me. I cannot believe you remember that conversation about my ancestors."

"Of course I remember. It was so important to you that you were looking for a sign, remember?"

"Oh, yes, I remember."

Eli's maternal grandfather, Dalton Livingston Duncan had fallen in love with Deborah Lee White, my great grandmother. They had met at Willard Psychiatric Hospital. After spending much of last year piecing together my own story, it turned out that my story is connected to Eli's story, much to our shock. That discovery was the rather significant *sign* for both of us. It was shortly after that discovery that Eli asked me to marry him.

"So what do you think of *Ruth* as a middle name for our daughter?" I ask.

"What if it turns out to be a boy?"

"Hmmmm, well, rather than Christina Ruth Fisher, I suppose we could name him Christian Kennedy Fisher, as in Anthony Kennedy."

Eli laughs at that.

"Ruth is a perfect name. In fact, I am remembering the sermon on Ruth I preached that day you came to church, the second time, I believe. I always felt those two things were not coincidental, that you and Ruth are somehow tied together."

"Yes, you always told me that I have a lot in common with Ruth."

"She had to leave her country and go to a different land, in much the same way that Naomi did earlier. You were transported from your birthplace in Mississippi, to your adoptive parents in Newark Valley, in much the same way that your grandmother was earlier. Deborah White was born in Willard, New York, and was adopted by a couple from Mississippi. You do have to admit that all those details are amazing."

"I do admit that, Eli. And in these past few months, I have even come to believe that God has something in store for me or for us. Just imagine how far that is for me to come, from not giving much thought to God at all, to suddenly believing that I am somehow special in God's eyes."

Eli nods, and I can tell he has other thoughts that he is thinking, but not sharing with me. I do not ask him what they are. Maybe I am too afraid to know.

+++++

I decided that I could wait until my birthday on April 6, but no longer than that to tell the world of my pregnancy. Today is that day.

Alberta is already in the kitchen when Eli and I come in. She gives me a big hug saying, "Happy Birthday, Del".

"Thank you," I grin, pleased that she has remembered. I turn 41 on this day.

"We have some news to share, Mom," Eli says. She looks worried, as if she expects to hear that we are moving to California, or some such thing.

"Don't look worried, Mom, it's good news!"

"So don't keep me in suspense," she moans.

I thought I should be the one to say it, so I just blurted out, "We're having a baby!"

"Oh, my God, are you sure? How far along are you? How did it happen?"

"We are certain that Del got pregnant on our wedding night. As to *how*, you'll just have to use your imagination on that one. That makes the due date around mid-September."

"I am so thrilled. Can you even imagine how thrilled Sebastian will be?" he beams. "We never even dared to dream this might happen. Everything has happened so quickly."

"Yes, it has," I agree.

"I was around your same age when Eli was born," Alberta comments. "You must be at least three months along by now, right?"

"Yes, and I have had a really easy pregnancy so far. No morning sickness. No problems. In fact, I feel better than I have every felt in my life," I add, which is the truth.

"I'm so glad," Alberta responds, tears in the corner of her eyes.

"I'm taking a breakfast tray to Sebastian, would you two like to come along and break the news?" she suggests.

"Great idea," Eli says.

The three of us enter Sebastian's room. He is already sitting in his chair, where he takes his meals. His world has shrunk, from a career with far flung influence and eloquent court arguments, to a battle confined to a few square feet.

"Well, this is an honor," he smiles. His speech is much slower, but not yet slurred, which is something that can happen, as his disease progressed. "So what is the occasion for this threesome?"

"We have great news, Dad," Eli says.

"We are having a baby," I add. I have only ever called him Sebastian. In light of the fact that I have both adoptive parents, and biological parents, adding another *Dad* to the mix just seemed overload. Sebastian and Alberta understood.

Sebastian beams. "Well, thank God for that. I am so happy for you, for all of us. When is our baby due?"

"Mid-September," Eli answers.

"I hope I live to see the day," Sebastian adds, this time with tears brimming, but not spilling.

"We hope so, too, Dad."

"Please stick around Sebastian, and meet your grand-daughter," I remark.

"And you already know that it is a girl?" he asks.

"Not officially, but if you believe in dreams, then we're sure. We each had different dreams about her. But we'll know soon enough."

"I'm going to try my best to be around to meet her," Sebastian says.

"Her name is Christina," Eli adds.

"Christina Fisher," Sebastian repeats. Hearing him say her name gives her even more substance and reality than she already has in my mind.

Eli gives him the full name, "Christina Ruth Fisher."

"So be it." Sebastian says.

CHAPTER 14

SEPTEMBER 14, 2008

I have not had any difficulties with my pregnancy. Considering that this is my first pregnancy, and I am forty one years old, that has been somewhat surprising to my doctor, Dr. Morris, who has worried about all sorts of things. She was especially shocked when I declined her suggestion of an amniocentesis, which could have ruled out Down's Syndrome. As far as I am concerned, five months into a pregnancy, when the test is given, is too far along to take such a test.

Given my risk factors, I have been monitored closely all along the way. No abnormalities or distress of mother or child have been evident. It has been a breeze. I feel a little worried about that, and fear that since the pregnancy has been so easy, the birth may well be especially difficult. But I will focus on having the most positive experience.

Of course, Eli has read everything he can get his hands on dealing with both pregnancy, childbirth and infancy. He has always been one to be prepared. The same week we discovered my pregnancy, he bought a copy of *What to Expect When You Are Expecting.* I cannot even guess how many books he has read on both pregnancy and childbirth. I have not read as diligently as he has.

Now that I am full term, and due at any moment, I will confess to the challenges of getting up and down, and tying my shoes. I used to enjoy an occasional hot bubble bath, but now I only take showers, because it is too hard to get in and out of the tub. I do enjoy the thrill of the new life growing and kicking inside of me, but I cannot say that I love the view of my body in the mirror. Not so with Eli. He loves my pregnant look, and is completely in awe of the whole process. He likes to put his ear to my pregnant belly and listen. Once when I asked him what he expected to hear, he smiled and said, "Daddy."

Eli will make a great father. He is gentle and compassionate, attentive and involved. This child is very blessed to have such a father. I cannot say the same for her mother, as her mother has some uncertainties about her family background and genetic history. I don't worry about that obsessively, but some concern has crossed my mind.

Suddenly, I think of my biological father, Cardinal Philippe Dominico Crechea Conti. Visiting him last year at the University of Rome and meeting him is something I shall never forget. Despite the shock of my appearing there on his doorstep, so to speak, he handled it so well, with both grace and dignity, greeting me with warmth. It was not at all what I had expected.

I learned that Crechea is his mother's maiden name. Unbelievably, the Cardinal's mother, who is in her eighties, is still living. With a twinkle in his eye, Cardinal Conti said he was going to tell her that she has a granddaughter. I cannot help but wonder whether or not he actually did that. I was amazed that he would even entertain such a notion, and decided that he must have an exceptional relationship with his mother.

When the young Italian met my mother Iris, he was using only his two middle names—Dominico Crechea. She called him Nico for short. I think of him now as Cardinal Conti, after uncovering all of his names. I do feel an emotional connection to him, but I do not consciously think of him as my father, since my Dad, Frank Williams, raised me and is still an active part of my life. If circumstances had been different, and Nico and Iris had stayed together, I'm sure he would have been a good father like Eli will be. I cannot even fathom how that might have affected who I am, or might have become.

The closer we have gotten to our due date, the more energy Alberta seems to have. We have settled nicely into the Fisher mansion in Chittenango. Over these past six months, Sebastian has become much weaker and now has difficulty with his motor skills. Alberta has brought in a day nurse and a night nurse. She has also set up a bed in Sebastian's study, and she now sleeps there. We have the entire upstairs of the house to ourselves. We do see Alberta in the kitchen early in the morning for coffee. She eats lightly, usually toast or bran cereal, but doesn't cook.

Since I stopped working at the law firm when I was six months pregnant, I became much more interested in food and in cooking and in nutrition. I have spent a great deal of time these past three months reading cookbooks, often of the organic or vegetarian kind. While I have never been a vegetarian before, I have been moving that direction for a while. It never ceases to amaze me how many new cooking avenues there are out there, if one commits to cooking without meat. Alberta says that I am now the queen of the kitchen and she has bequeathed it to me in its entirety. I am still learning my way around. I do appreciate feeling as if it belongs to me. That is liberating.

Alberta always asks about my pregnancy, and she also remembers when she too was pregnant with Eli, about the same age as I am now. I know she worries, because with Eli she had a long and difficult labor lasting for thirty six hours. We both know that Sebastian's remaining days are likely few, but that is not something we ever discuss.

My actual due date is September 17. It is getting closer. Today I stayed home from church. I certainly enjoy going to church, and now feel very welcome by the parishioners. But at this point, of course, whenever anyone looks at me all they can think of is . . . . are you still *here*?

I just wanted to avoid that scene today. I guess they are all tired of waiting, as I am. I am anxious to meet this new member of our family.

When Eli got home, I asked him to tell me all about the morning. He always arrives at the church by eight o'clock. The custodian has already unlocked the church and taken care of whatever doors or heating or cooling systems need tending. At nine o'clock, Eli teaches a Bible Study class, which is attended by about twenty people. I've been to that class before, and I like the fact that he does not lecture, but leads a discussion. Most of the time, they study the lectionary scriptures assigned for the particular Sunday of the church year. Today is the start-up of the Sunday School program after summer recess. Eli said that the attendance was really great today at both the Christian Education classes and worship. He has only been at this church for about three years. It has grown significantly since he came. Eli has a lot of charisma. I have no doubt that the ladies must find him most appealing. I know I do. Fortunately, I am not jealous of the other women's interest in him. I understand that people are drawn to the light in his spirit. The good looks and charm are just extras. I'm not sure how he managed to stay single and also celibate for so long.

I certainly look forward to when we can make love again, after the birth. I think I must be abnormal, since I have had fierce sexual hunger for the first six months of my pregnancy. That was certainly a surprise to Eli. He found no references to that in his books, but he never turned down my constant demands.

I feel some pain in my lower back. Considering the weight I am carrying around in the front, that is really not surprising. I do not think I will mention it to Eli. I am sure he would only worry.

Chapter 15

Monday, September 15, 2008

"Del, how are you feeling?" Eli asks, after I am out of the shower and wrapped in a towel, as far as it will go around the front.

"Other than some back pain, I think I'm fine. But I've had some back pain all along," I assure him.

"I think I am going to stay home today."

"Eli, I don't really think there is any reason for that just yet, unfortunately."

"The waiting must be really hard."

"Yes, it is. The waiting and the mobility issues, and the unknowns," I add.

"Well, I am definitely not going in to the office this morning. In fact, Mom said she thinks I should not go into the office at all this week. She is also concerned about Dad. Sometimes he is confused, you know Del. But when he is lucid, he always asks how you are coming along."

"Do you think it would be all right if I visited with him today?"

"It certainly cannot do any harm."

"Maybe I'll go right after breakfast." Eli decides that he will let me go by myself, just in case there might be anything Sebastian might want to say to me. I think that is considerate of him though I cannot imagine it.

When the day nurse sees me at the door, she smiles and says, "He's awake and seems to be quite alert today. Please come in." When I stepped in, she left the room.

"Hi, Sebastian," I greet.

"Oh, it's Del. Come closer, dear. I am so happy to see you." His speech is somewhat slurred, but I can understand every word.

"How's my granddaughter?"

"I think she should be coming soon, Sebastian."

Of course it was confirmed early on that our fetus is a girl, though we had known early in the pregnancy. We both had dreams to that effect. I wonder if Eli has shared that with Sebastian.

"Oh, good."

"How are you feeling?" I ask.

"Like my time here on earth is limited."

"Are you afraid of death?" I wonder, not at all sure if that was an appropriate question.

"Not at all. In fact, for the past few days, I'm sure that I have been visited by angels."

"Really? Have they revealed any secrets that I would want to know?"

"Yes, as a matter of fact." I had not expected him to say that, and am taken back.

"Such as?" I wonder, though he did not immediately answer my question.

"I seem to experience the angels mostly when I am floating between being awake and being asleep. One of them is *my* angel. Not the angel of death, but just one assigned to me."

"That's interesting," I think out loud, fascinated.

"That one is a female." I smile at that.

"How many are there?" I ask.

"At least three. I think they are loved ones from the other side, maybe people I knew or loved."

"And what have you learned."

"My lady angel says that Christina will be special."

"Of course she will be. She's your granddaughter," I say. Suddenly a shooting pain struck along my lower back. This is not something I have felt before, and it makes me wonder.

"More than that."

"What do you mean?"

"Special abilities," Sebastian says, stringing that out slowly. I am afraid to ask what he means, so I do not say anything. He is speaking with effort now. "I wish I could tell you more."

"That's okay. Please don't exert yourself too much," I suggest. We sit together in silence then for a while. Within a few minutes Sebastian seems to get a second wind, and wants to talk some more. He speaks slowly and deliberately, only slightly slurred, so I can understand him.

"As an adult, I never practiced any religion. But I grew up Catholic. Even Alberta and Eli don't know this, but when I was a youngster, I wanted to be a priest. For a while, that's what I thought I would do." I know that Eli will be shocked by that revelation.

"Oh, my goodness, that is a surprise. What happened?"

"Life happened." I was thinking that Sebastian may have realized that he could not live a life of celibacy. He could tell that was what I was thinking from the nodding of my head. Then he added this: "I had a close encounter with a priest I would not want to be."

"Oh, I'm sorry." A different image creeps into my mind. It is a shocking one.

"Up to that point, I took my religion very seriously. In fact, Eli is actually named after the biblical prophet."

I am very surprised to hear this. "Does he know that? He never told me there was an intentional connection."

"I don't think he does know that. Even Alberta does not know about my childhood fantasy of the priesthood."

"May I ask why?"

"I never wanted to reveal my experience with the priest. I was too ashamed."

"Thank you for telling me." And I did feel honored. "Sebastian, considering all of that, how did you feel about Eli going into the ministry?"

"Well, at first, I was utterly amazed. It felt almost like an act of the universe. I had not done what I was called to do, and so that fell to the next generation.

Then after a while, I just became incredibly proud of my son."

"Did you tell him that?" I ask. It has always seemed to me like Eli is uncertain about how his parents feel about his ministry.

"I guess I just always thought he knew. I have always been proud of everything he has done. When you came along, Del, I knew that you were the one for him. And I knew that something was happening to my family. I knew the first time I met you."

"Meeting Eli and being part of your family has certainly changed my life, to put it mildly."

"The biggest changes will come with Christina."

"I wish I knew what you mean," I answer. But I did not yet know what being a parent will be like.

"Don't worry," Sebastian comforts.

"I can't really remember, Sebastian. Did I ever tell you Christina's middle name?" I ask.

"Probably, but I don't recall."

"Ruth," I answer. A big smile spread across Sebastian's face, as if that pleased him enormously. "For Ruth Bader Ginsburg."

I tell Sebastian that we decided to continue the family tradition of naming our child after a Supreme Court Justice, which had been the family tradition for Eli and Sebastian and at least two prior generations.

"That's nice," he says, as if he is thinking of something else. I can tell that he is growing weary. He has already talked more than I would have anticipated. I decide to leave him to rest.

"Thanks for talking to me, Sebastian. Maybe Christina Ruth Fisher will be along soon. I hope so."

I lean over, holding my belly with one arm, and kiss him on the forehead.

CHAPTER 16

THE BIRTH

It is nine o'clock at night. We have just called Dr. Morris to let her know that I am likely in labor. I have been having back pain, but do not recognize it as labor. Eli suspects that it is. My contractions, if you can call them that, are coming ten minutes apart. Dr. Morris said that when they were five minutes apart that I should go to the hospital and let her know when we are on the way. At eleven o'clock, Eli calls the doctor back and says he was getting nervous and that we are headed to the hospital shortly, even though the contractions are not yet five minutes apart. Eli put my small piece of luggage containing the necessities in the car. He also has an emergency bag he had packed which he places on the back floorboard of the car. So far, I am not feeling any major pain. I can tell something is happening, but it does not feel like hard labor. Eli takes charge.

"Del, I want you to ride in the back seat, just in case."

"Just in case of what?" I protest.

"In case I have an accident or something like that. I want to keep you and the baby safe." Once I am in the back seat and Eli is driving, I am glad for the extra room, because the labor pains pick up in intensity and I move around trying to find a comfortable position. Not ever having been in labor before, I do not know exactly what to expect. I also assume that everyone's experience is different.

Suddenly there is one long contraction with no letup. My water breaks. Eli is driving past DeWitt on Rt. 5. I believe that he has just made the entrance to Route 481. I need him to stop and help.

"Eli, you have to help. Something is happening." I cry out. I lay down in the back seat, moaning now. I am wearing a loose fitting dress, thankfully. There is this huge pressure between my legs. I cannot believe this is happening to me.

"Eli help me please," I plead.

"Two minutes, Del," he says. I am completely taken over by labor pains, but try not to panic.

Soon, I feel Eli pull the car off the road. I do not know where we are, because I am lying down. Within moments, he opens the back door. Eli takes the bag off of the floor board and opens it.

"I have to call 911," he says.

"There's no time, Eli. You have to do something." I can see the look on my poor husband's face. He is so worried. But knowing my husband, Eli has thought about this as a possibility. One never knows, and he likes to be prepared, good Eagle Scout that he is.

Eli lifts my dress and cut off my underwear with a pair of scissors on both sides, but not near the birth site. He slides a clean white sheet underneath my legs and bottom. I try not to cry out from the pain.

There is the light from the car ceiling, but it is not very bright. I can tell that there is also some light coming from outside the car, but I do not know what it is. Eli has prepared for every contingency. He slips over his forehead a head lantern like the ones that miners use which will shine a light and leave his hands free. I chuckle when I see that.

"There's a head here!" he says with excitement in his voice. I can also hear the shock.

"I have to push," I grit my teeth, moaning.

"The head is coming out." Eli has tears streaming down his face now. "Can you push some more?"

I think my husband is hurting more than I am. He groans. I push. With a few more great pushing efforts, the baby slides out into Eli's hands. Despite his excitement and through his tears, he even has the presence of mind to look at his watch. I am suddenly so exhausted that I cannot move. Eli wraps our little baby girl in a soft white receiving blanket he had brought in his emergency bag, just in case. He clears out her mouth and nose with a small syringe. He begs, "Breathe, Christina, breathe!" And she does, wailing only briefly to announce her arrival. After that, he lays the baby on my chest and with his shaking hands he dials 911. Then I watch as he removes a new white shoelace from a package and wraps it around the umbilical cord and ties a knot.

Suddenly I have the presence of mind enough to wonder where we are exactly. On what thoroughfare has this monumental event taken place?

"Where are we Eli," I ask.

"When you asked me to help, Del, we were already on Rt. 481 South, so I turned off at the Jamesville Road exit, and of course, within half a mile you turn into the church parking lot." We are at our church, Eli's church. I can hardly believe it.

I cannot help but laugh out loud. Here we are again, back where it had all started, back where she had started. Conceived in the pastor's study, born in a Toyota Camry in the same church's parking lot. What could be more perfect? It crosses my mind that God has a sense of humor.

Shortly after Eli has done everything he can do, an ambulance pulls into the driveway. The medics asked him questions. When they ask what time the baby was born, I hear him say, "12:03" That means that it is Tuesday. At least, I am able to recognize that fact, and think to myself—Tuesday's child, full of grace.

Christina and I are then transported to University Hospital to take care of all the other necessary medical functions. We are both in very good shape. We are admitted to the hospital and both checked out. It takes some time to go through the entire process, for paperwork, and visits by pediatrician and obstetrician. By Wednesday morning, they are willing to let us go home. Christina Ruth Fisher has certainly made an entrance that her parents are not likely to soon forget.

When Dr. Morris stops by to see me, she just shakes her head. "So you couldn't wait for me!"

"I guess not," I answer, smiling. I am proud of myself, though I had not intentionally chosen to bypass the hospital.

"Eli did a great job, you know Del." He has gone home temporarily to change clothes, and take a shower, but will return in an hour or two.

"So I've heard. After he delivered Christina, he confessed that he had watched at least twenty videos on how to deliver a baby." I had not known how worried he was about that.

"Talk about being prepared!"

"That's Eli. He also had with him everything that he might need. I wonder whether or not we might have made it to the hospital if he had not been so well prepared. There's that self-fulfilling prophecy thing."

"Well, it sounds to me like you had a very short labor. No one could have predicted that."

"I am thinking now that the back pains I had the day before must have been labor pains, but they did not feel like labor pains."

"Yes, I am sure they were. If you ever plan to have another baby, you might also expect a short labor, so don't wait around. Oh, and I saw Dr. Robbins in the nursery. Dr. Robbins is the pediatrician on call tonight. Christina looks perfect. Seven pounds exactly. Lots of dark hair. They'll probably bring her around soon for a feeding. Are you ready for that?"

"Oh, yes." I smile at the thought.

Shortly after Dr. Morris leaves, a nurse brings me my baby girl, wrapped tightly in her swaddling, as all newborns are. I need to look at her from head to toe and count fingers and toes, which I have not yet done. It had been dark and visibility was poor in the car. The medics held her during the ambulance ride. This is my first chance.

I am looking at her tiny toenails when I notice the bottom of her right foot. There is a bright red birthmark there, roughly the shape of a plus sign. Although the edges are poorly defined, it is clear. The center of the sign is right in the middle of her foot, and its arms radiate upward, downward, and to each side. I feel a moment of relief and gratitude. Thank goodness that such a mark is on the bottom of her foot, and not somewhere more visible. In fact, I think to myself that the bottom of her foot is the perfect place for such a mark.

No sooner do I have my newborn baby at my breast than she locks on to my nipple, as if she knows exactly what she is supposed to do, and she does it with skill and gusto. I marvel at the simple miracle that a child is born with a sucking instinct. I have read that nursing is sometimes difficult, and have been warned by the nurse of the same possibility. But there are no difficulties for Christina and me. It is a life giving and natural instinct of nature that we both enjoy.

Chapter 17

A New Direction

By the time we are released on Wednesday morning, I am feeling great. Christina has moments of alertness, others of sleep, some of nursing, but mostly she just seems content to be alive and in the world.

I ride in the back seat with Christina, as Eli drives carefully home. She rides in her infant car seat, sleeping peacefully. At home, she will sleep in the cradle in our bedroom at first, though we have prepared for her a beautiful nursery, with all the trimmings. I have chosen yellow and white for the color scheme, not wanting to spend a lot of time with pink.

We have received so many lovely gifts from both friends of the Fishers, of which there are many, as well as members of the Community Church. The church gave us a shower, and we both attended. There is another family that claims us, to whom we belong.

The cradle has been in the family for several generations. It is made of wood, and swings back and forth. I have it placed near my side of the bed, where I can easily rock the cradle, or take Christina out of the cradle and nurse her. We are as prepared as any parents could be.

Alberta greets us beaming. "Let me see that precious little bundle." I hand Christina to her grandmother Fisher. I cannot help but think of my own mother Williams, and how thrilled she would have been to experience this moment. When it comes to my own parentage, I have two biological and two adoptive. I think of each of them in whatever circumstances their memories are triggered. I have no memory of my biological mother Iris, but I have many memories now of Granny Grace, who cared for me the first five years of my life. Those memories have now returned after being repressed for many years, due to the trauma of her death.

As I look at my tiny daughter and her peaceful face, I hope and pray that her life will not be filled with as much loss as mine. For my first five years of my life, I was happy. Then after my grandmother's death, I was sad and withdrawn for a while, until I was adopted by Frank and Ida Williams. Then I was happy again, repressing my early years.

By the time I unraveled all of that, I had met Eli, and he provided the comfort and strength that I have needed. I do hope that what I have given to him comes somewhere close to matching what he has given to me. But everything is different now that Christina Ruth Fisher has been born. We three are one. A unit.

A family. My own family. We married quickly. I conceived quickly and soon, here we all are.

Alberta could not take her eyes off of the baby. Since Eli was an only child, I know that she has not had the chance to nurture and fuss over a little girl.

When Eli comes in through the door, he immediately asks about his father, because he knows that Sebastian has been failing, even since the day before. "Mom, how is Dad doing?"

"He is weak today, having trouble breathing, but determined to see this child. You and Del will need to take her into his room and introduce her to him before waiting too long."

"We will, Mom," Eli assures.

There are quite a few things to unload from the car. We did take the time to take all the baby things upstairs to our quarters, or at least Eli took them upstairs. I wait with Alberta in the kitchen. We talked about our birth experiences. Mine and hers could not be more opposite. Hers lasted for many hours, and the birth itself was also difficult. I was not even aware that my body was in labor, and the birth came very quickly. She laughed when I told her the story of Christina's birth. I'm sure she had heard Eli's version the night before, but mine has a different slant, to say the least. I am drinking a cup of coffee while she holds the baby. Eli returns from emptying the car and carrying it upstairs.

"Are you ready, Del? We need to go and see Dad."

"Yes, I'm ready," I answer. "Alberta, are you coming with us."

"I think I'll let this be your own private time with Sebastian. There may not be any other opportunities," she says. I am shocked to hear her say that. Eli does not appear to be surprised.

Sebastian had been propped up in the bed by his nurse, and is clearly waiting for us. He does not have much color, and his breathing is labored. He is wearing an oxygen tube in his nose. Despite all that, his joy at seeing us is unmistakable.

"Eli, Del, I am so happy to see you," Sebastian struggles to say. "May I see the baby?"

Eli takes the baby from me and holds her up right over Sebastian's chest, so that he can easily see her. Both father and son know that he is too weak to hold her.

"Perfect," he smiles, looking at the newborn.

"Yes, she is," Eli affirms.

"I am so proud of you, son," Sebastian says, surprising Eli.

"Thanks, Dad, that means a lot." I see Eli's eyes fill with tears, but he keeps them in check, I know with great effort.

Then he looks at me and his eyes are intense. He struggles to speak, but I can understand him. "Del, Christina is your double portion."

I see a stunned look on Eli's face. With great effort, Sebastian gets out one more sentence, before his eyes close in exhaustion.

"I'm so glad that I have lived to see her; now I can rest in peace."

++

Later, when we are settled in our rooms upstairs, and Christina is in her cradle, Eli and I sit together on the bed.

"Del, do you remember the Elijah story, and what you told me about your grandmother's death?"

"Yes, of course."

"And do you remember what you thought you heard her say?" he asks.

"I heard her say, *You are Elisha.*"

"Yes, part of the story of Elijah is that at his death, Elisha asked God for a double portion of Elijah's gifts as a prophet."

"I am familiar with the story, but I don't know what it has to do with us," I say.

"Well, frankly, I am trying to figure that out too," Eli responds. "My father said that Christina is the double portion, or more specifically, our double portion. First, I didn't know he was even familiar with that story. And second, I wonder—did you ever tell him about your experience at your grandmother's death."

"No, of course not."

"Well, I never told him either. So how did he know?"

"Well, Eli, what do you make of it?" I ask.

"I can only think that somehow, as he prepares to pass over to the other side, he has tapped into some knowledge from beyond this world. You and I have both tried to understand what that event meant in your life. We have probably both interpreted it in different ways. I figured that it meant you would have a specific ministry of your own someday."

"Yes, I realize that has been your interpretation. But honestly, that never made any sense to me. I don't come from the kind of background that would lead me in that direction."

"That would not have stopped God."

"Eli, I have even looked into the courses at Colgate Rochester seminary, wondering if I should go that direction. And I still may take a course there someday, but certainly not for a while."

"Maybe that's not the right direction," Eli says.

"Christina is our direction."

"Yes. And if she is also our double portion, that could mean that she is the one who will pick up the cloak and do God's work."

"Let's just let her find her own way, Eli," I suggest. I am no biblical scholar, but I know enough to realize that the lives of prophets are not always easy. I do not want her life to be hard.

CHAPTER 18

SEPTEMBER 18, 2008

Sebastian Fisher died in his sleep during the night. It happened only hours after he met Christina. Eli and I believe that he did exactly what he wanted to do, which was to wait for her arrival.

Alberta is as calm as she can be, under the circumstances. She has just been through the news of both a birth and a death practically on the same day. Although she is well into her eighties, Alberta seems strong and determined. There are all sorts of people in and out of the house: Nurses, Hospice workers, the funeral director, the coroner. Sebastian has left clear directions about his wishes, so there is no guesswork. He does not want a traditional funeral service. Instead, he wants a reception at their home at some later time. He wants to be cremated with his ashes scattered about the estate.

I have been focused on holding and nursing Christina. Alberta is in charge of all the arrangements. Eli and I decide that we will shorten our baby's name to Chrissy when we speak of her. That has one less syllable. In its written form, her name will always be Christina. Chrissy reminds me somewhat of my own early childhood name, Cressie. I hold her and she stares into my eyes. I am enthralled by the deep purity in the eyes of a newborn, a wellspring of innocence. It makes my heart spasm just to look at her. I can tell already in these few short hours that I have strong maternal instincts—to love unconditionally, to protect fiercely, to nurture fully.

Eli and Alberta begin to look at the calendar for a potential date for Sebastian's Memorial Reception. They want to wait for several weeks to pass, so that Christina is somewhat older, before making a public appearance. We might want to show her off to some of the guests, if she was agreeable during that time. Saturday, October 11 is selected. Alberta calls the string ensemble from the Syracuse Symphony to check the date with them. She also checks with her caterer. The major pieces of the plan are beginning to fall into place.

"Mom, you don't have to do all of this today," Eli says.

"I know. But what else would I do?" Alberta answers.

Eli later shares his thoughts with me. He realizes that the form and shape of Alberta's days, which revolved around Sebastian's illness, are no longer in place. It is at least a double loss—the loved one and the companionship, the familiar battle with the disease and the structure of her days. Eli has dealt with grief and loss for years, in his ministry. This is different. This is the end of an era, a generation, a giant of a man. This is deeply personal. He will miss his father so much, Eli suddenly realizes. He says he needs some time alone to process all that has happened.

I watch through the window as Eli walks around the tree filled lawn. I wonder if he notices that the leaves are already beginning to change color. It seems too early for that.

It sometimes feels like we have lived our lives on fast forward, as the seasons flew by.

Later that night, I wanted to make love to comfort Eli. I was still sore from the birth of our child, and thought that it might not be wise, nor even feasible. At first, Eli was reluctant. But he was suddenly overcome by all the emotion that he had endured in the last few days, and he could not hold himself back. It was a raw mixture of pain and pleasure, relatives of birth and death. And it brought out all the tears and anguish that Eli had been holding back. This was not like any experience I have known before. This was precipitated as much by loss as by desire. In the end, it was about the desire to live. It was a matter of holding on to the very essence of life.

When Eli's sobs finally subsided, I pulled his head to my chest, and he was comforted.

+

Christina's cries sound more like calls than shrieking unhappy wails. She seems to want to communicate with me, or with us, but without the need to scream. It is about six o'clock in the morning. I have brought her to our bed and am feeding her. Eli suddenly wakes up and sits up. He takes in the sight of the two of us, and smiles. I can tell that he is remembering the recent events. He seems confused.

"What day is it?" he asks.

"Friday."

"Oh, my," he says. "I have done nothing to prepare for Sunday."

"Well, could you get someone else to cover for you?"

"Not at this late date."

"Maybe you could just wing it," I suggest.

"Now there's a thought!" he responds. "But you know me, I like to be prepared."

"Eli, your father has just died. Your wife has just had a baby. Give yourself a break!

Are you really planning to be there on Sunday?"

"Yes, I want to be there. Not that I have any idea at the moment what I might say. But you're right, Del. If ever there is a time to "wing it", this would be it."

Then Eli gets a strange smile on his face, as if he has thought of something funny.

"What are you thinking?"

"About the meaning of winging it."

"Well, doesn't it mean, just go with the flow, and be spontaneous."

"Well, in this case, I think it just might mean something different."

"Such as?"

"Leaving it up to the Holy Spirit," he says. "Remember the wings, the fluttering wings of your childhood."

"Yes, I remember."

"Well, winging it for me right now means letting it go, turning it over, trusting God's Spirit."

"Is that what you plan to do?"

"I think so. I have done that before, and I know that I can do it. I don't usually, because God and I meet as much in the preparation as in the delivery. I love that process. It's like a conversation, a give and take, a back and forth."

"You've never told me that before." I comment.

"I know."

"You know what I think, Eli?"

"What's that?"

"I think that if you wing it, it will be like a dance with the Holy Spirit."

"You may be right. You've experienced that dance, haven't you?"

"Yes, most recently at my grandmother's monument. It was a wonderful spiritual experience."

"Is there anything else you can tell me about that?"

"It was purifying. I left a lot of baggage there."

"You mean healing."

"Yes, I suppose what they say about that place is true."

"I love you Del," Eli says suddenly. "And thank you for last night. I must have had a lot of stored up physical need."

"I believe it was actually more spiritual."

Eli looks at me with love in his eyes.

CHAPTER 19

ELIJAH'S MESSAGE, AS SHARED WITH DEL

As some of you may already know, this has been a monumental week in my life. So in that spirit, I am going to do something different this morning. I am going to simply talk to you. First, let me share with you something personal about my process of sermon preparation and delivery. You may have noticed that I have a strong preference for following the liturgical calendar, those scriptures which follow the life of Christ. In fact, mentors have suggested to me that to do otherwise is an exercise in self-indulgence.

If I chose only to speak on whatever theme or topic interested me at the moment, then I would be focusing on my own agenda, my own biases. The discipline of following lectionary scriptures keeps me on the right track.

In case everyone does not know, this week, Del gave birth to our daughter Christina. I am sure that most of you have heard by now, as that kind of news travels fast. And my beloved father Sebastian passed away the next day. That is where my heart and soul and mind have been these past few days—certainly not on preparing for worship.

Another thing that I want you to know, which probably comes from my Presbyterian background, is that I am not much of a believer in using the pulpit as a personal confessional. When a pastor divulges personal information, it does not take much before it is too much. Too much personal information is also directed toward self, not directed toward God's word. I certainly do use personal examples as illustrations, as long as they support the biblical theme and the message of the sermon.

On the other hand, I am sure there are those of you who might greatly prefer a pastor who practices personal witness. That is what I am going to do this morning. But being who I am, I do have to try to put it in the context of scripture. It was very easy for me to identify that scripture, because that one verse is one I have deeply internalized. It comes from 2 Corinthians, Chapter 3. Some of you will probably recognize it. In essence, it says that I am a letter of Christ, because the Spirit of the Living God is written on my heart. That describes me exactly, as I understand myself. I am God's etching, God's engraving, God's letter. And that is not really anything written on pages, or even captured within a Christian tradition, but it is written in my heart.

As our congregation, you all have shared in our pregnancy, as far as watching the growth that has taken place in Del's womb. That itself is an incredible miracle. Neither of us have been married before, nor had a child before, and now, in our forties, God chooses to give us a daughter. Of course, this makes me think about Abraham and Sarah, though we are not quite that old. It makes me think of Elizabeth and Zechariah, to whom a child was given late in life. God's word has been written in all of our lives, from the beginning of time. I see God as the Author. We are the story.

On Monday evening, Del began having severe back pains. We did not experience what you might call the normal kind of labor. She certainly did not recognize her pains as getting her closer to delivery. That being the case, we did not make it to the hospital. Thankfully, I had insisted that Del ride in the back seat so she would have more room and be more comfortable. The trip from our house in Chittenango was fairly uneventful. But by the time we got to DeWitt and I had just turned onto Rt. 481 south headed toward the hospital, Del said she needed help. I drove for a few more miles, wanting very badly to make it to the hospital. She said she needed my help immediately. I realized that I was not very far from our church. I pulled into the parking lot here, and by the light shining from the steeple, I delivered our child Christina.

In case you are wondering how I did that, let me confess that I watched about twenty videos on *how to deliver a child*, which I found on the internet. Christina was born shortly after midnight on Tuesday of this week. Thankfully, there were no complications, and I did not make any terrible mistakes, and both Del and Christina are doing wonderfully well. I called 911 and an ambulance soon arrived and took mother and infant to University Hospital. I followed along behind the ambulance.

After just a few days, I can already tell you that I am going to be a different person as a result of becoming a father. Strange and powerful emotions stir in one's soul when you become a parent. I think as all of that unfolds over time, I will understand God much better than I did before. God loves the children of God's own creation, but when they become adults, God does not make their choices for them. I can only wonder whether or not God feels anguish, or disappointment, pride or joy. I am sure that God has a very different perspective from the one we have. I still believe that God *feels*. God is love. Love is not entirely about feelings, but feelings are certainly a part of love. So is sacrifice, and joy. So is the need to teach and correct and protect. I have so much yet to learn. And I am sure that Christina will have much to teach me too.

+

My father Sebastian said months ago that he hoped that he would live to meet his grandchild. And he did just that. He gazed upon her and said that now he could go in peace. And that also is just exactly what he did. I find it miraculous that he managed to hold on until just past her birth. No doubt, God had a hand in that, but so also did my father's determination and his will.

Several hours after he met Christina, my Dad left this world for a place in a better one, which God has prepared for us all. I learned some important things about my father during this process. For one thing, I learned that even though he has never been a practicing Christian as an adult, he was nevertheless a man of faith. I was shocked to learn that as young child, he had considered the priesthood. I was amazed to discover that he has always been proud of me and my ministry. And perhaps, most surprising of all, I learned that I was named after the prophet Elijah from the Old Testament. Names are important. They frequently are determiners of one's direction in life, one's choices, one's identity, one's destiny. I am intrigued with the notion that even though I did not realize that my name was biblical, I found my way to this particular path. Since my parents were not church attenders, the odds were certainly against that. But the right mentors came along to direct me and encourage me.

I am not the same person today that I was last Sunday. And honestly, I think that is exactly God's plan for all of us, that we have experiences, that we learn, succeed and fail, grow in spirit, that we are better this week than last.

This week, I have been especially struck by the connection between life and death, between being born and dying. They are both part of the same process. I don't really think that life is a straight line with a mark for the beginning and another mark for the end. I think life is a circle, or many circles with no beginning and no end. It is a circle that is wrapped around all that life has to offer, encompassing pain and disease, order and messiness, love and disaster. Joy and grief.

Those are the two things that marked my week. Joy and grief. Joy at the birth of my daughter. Grief at the loss of my father, whom I have always admired and loved. His exit was long and drawn out as he fought Parkinson's Disease. But he had the ending that he wanted, a view of what comes next. He was surrounded by those who love him most. We are planning the celebration that he wanted us to have.

There are no words for the joy that I feel from the experience of birth. I cannot imagine that anyone could go through that without shedding tears. It is deeply profound. It could well be that it was more profound for me because I was intimately involved. But I have no doubt that any witness to the occasion of birth would be so moved.

I think about the coincidence, the God-incidence of our infant's birth happening in the church parking lot. That is a rather humble place. I do remember being aware of the light from the steeple, and also noticing the beautiful starry sky that night.

So out of all of this, I do want to share some lessons that I have learned.

One might be that *all things are connected.* We are all part of this infinite universe. It is a dynamic, living, organic thing, both at the level of the physical— mass and atoms and all of that, but also at the level of the spiritual—where mystical things take place, for which there is no logical explanation. The realm of the spiritual is just as real as the physical world. We may not have come up with rules and categories that apply to this realm, but it exists with as much certainty as the fact that you and I are sitting here this morning.

Another lesson that I could take from my experiences this week, *it is never too late.* In God's timing, it is never too late. At forty six years old, I did not expect to become a father for the first time. Or for that matter, to find the woman I would want to marry.

Del has suggested that *Ruth* be Christina's middle name. I think I was most keenly aware of Del the Sunday last year when I was preaching on the book of Ruth. The more I learned about Del's life story, the more similarities I could see between her and Ruth. What I also remember is that she had already left before I got a chance to speak with her that day. I was disappointed. Like everything else in God's world, that worked itself out.

We have chosen October 11 for the day our family will celebrate my father's life. And we have selected Sunday, October 12 for the day of our daughter's baptism. It makes sense to us for those two events to be linked together, as their birth and death were linked. I also believe that they will one day meet again.

In God's world, we can *expect the unexpected.* The resurrection is the perfect example of that. When it looked like everything was lost, that hatred and violence had prevailed, an amazing thing happened. The risen Christ appeared. He appeared enough times to his disciples that there was no doubt in their minds that it was real, that he had risen from the dead.

I believe that we can all rise from our own deaths as well. Some of those might include the end of a relationship, the end of a job, disappointment with one's career, being betrayed by a friend or lover. We can be crushed by the things that life throws our way. But Jesus' resurrection suggests that there really is no death, that we can start over again and again; that even when our bodies fail, there is another place, another time where loved ones await, where a reunion will take place, where the very One who made us will welcome us home. And what a day of rejoicing that will be.

++

Eli also reported to me his very strange, and unplanned ending to the service. He was unexpectedly overcome by words that are part of the celebration of communion, and although they were in no way connected to what he had just said, he was unable to keep himself from uttering them. In fact, he heard the words come from his mouth, but could not imagine that they were his.

We are all one in Jesus Christ, one in ministry together, until Christ comes in final victory. And so together today, we proclaim the mystery of faith:

It only took two seconds for the congregation to give the familiar response. They were more

accustomed to reading it, but still they knew the
words, and uttered them in unison:

> Christ has died; Christ is risen;
> Christ will come again.

Chapter 20

Sebastian's Reception

Alberta has received countless phone calls following Sebastian's death, many offering to help. There are also numerous cards and letters. Apparently, Sebastian had a commitment to pro bono work far beyond what his family had ever known. Alberta selected half a dozen of those recipients to help her with hosting duties. Each one of those invited was thrilled with the opportunity to repay in some small way, what had been done for them.

Since there are so many rooms in the house, and so many serving stations, Alberta wants to make sure that there is a host in each room to tend to the guests' needs. She communicated with each one of the hosts and hostesses via email, to explain her desires and needs. She also wants to make sure that each guest signs the guest book as they enter, so one young man, Jose` is assigned to that task at the front door. I enjoy talking to Jose` and can tell that he is clearly honored to be included in the Memorial Reception. Sebastian had defended him when he had simply been at the wrong place at the wrong time when a robbery took place. Jose` was exonerated and went on to become a high school science teacher. I wonder when I hear his story if Sebastian had kept track of all those he helped over the years.

For the last three and a half weeks, all of us have participated in preparing the photo boards. Those are assembled by the decades of Sebastian's life. The Photo Board from birth to ten years old resides in the formal living room. That is also where the musicians are placed to provide classical music. The teenage years' photo display is located in the den, and so forth. When I walk through there myself one time, I notice how Deborah White's large painting is inevitably a conversation piece. It is still unbelievable to me to consider that my great-grandmother's art ended up in Eli's den.

The decade of Sebastian's twenties is on exhibit in the library, his thirties in the small adjacent study. The middle aged version of this remarkable man is on a photo display in the dining room, and the older version in the small, but formal parlor. The Fisher house is one of those older homes with multiple rooms, each with a specific function. Given my own decorating choice, I think I am more inclined toward open space, but the room arrangement fits the character and architecture of the house. Surely a child will enjoy all of its nooks and crannies. Around every corner is another room.

During the past months, I have enjoyed doing some decorating upstairs on our wing of the house, putting together a nursery in particular. I chose a cheerful yellow and white color scheme, with splashes of apple green. Even though I have known that we were expecting a girl, I did not want to go with the traditional pink. I found a beautiful yellow, green and creamed-colored rug for the middle of the nursery. It ends up being a focal point in the room.

Eli gave me the green light to make whatever changes to our bedroom that I desired. In that room, I have brought many of the pale blue and yellow touches from my cottage, in the nick-nacks, the art pieces, and the curtains.

After the first two months of our marriage, I spend less and less time at my cottage, and have begun to emotionally detach from it. At one time, I put so much of myself into that little house, and loved it so much. In fact, I nurtured it with such tender care, that it clearly served as a substitute for the child that I did not have during those years. But now I understand that it represents my past, and that my future will be in the big house. Recently, I suggested to Eli that we put my house on the market. He was surprised by this suggestion and wants to make sure that I am ready and will not regret selling it.

Because the Photo Boards are in various rooms, guests are encouraged to go from room to room. In several of the rooms, there are also delicious hors d'oeuvres provided by the caterer. Sebastian had two siblings, neither of whom is still living, but several of their children, Eli's cousins, are attending the Memorial event. The family members are also scattered among the rooms. Alberta knows that I have to tend to the baby, so mercifully, she assigns me as a floater. It is a very impressive event, with well thought out details. Sebastian would be proud.

I make it a point to meet all the room hosts and ask them about their stories. Each one had an account of Sebastian's kindness to them, and how his intervention in their lives at a crucial and often terrifying moment, had been life changing. Later in his career, Sebastian was appointed as the Onondaga County District Attorney. Earlier he was a defense attorney, so he practiced law from both the defense and the prosecuting sides.

Even Alexander and Roxanne Golden attend the reception. I worked for their law firm for twenty years. It is good to see them. Both express how much they miss my efficient presence in their office. At six months pregnant, I decided that it was time to stay at home, and be there for Alberta and Sebastian and to take the best possible care of Christina, and also Eli. To be perfectly honest, my job in the law firm also felt more like the past than the future. I still do not know exactly what our future will look like, but I do know that the future is in the process of opening up before me.

I am glad that we have hired and trained an occasional nanny. During the reception, she has been directed to come and get me whenever Christina needs to be nursed, but for most of the duration of the reception I am able to float around from room to room and meet many of the guests. Eli is the most sought after figure of the day, as the only child. He is assigned to the living room, but I notice that he also floats to different locations. There are a couple of wine stations serving only New York State wine, exactly as Sebastian requested.

Judge Worley catches my eye and I go and give him a warm embrace. Worley officiated at our wedding on Christmas Eve last year. That was a joyful occasion for all of us who were there. I could not help but think that tomorrow will be an equally joyous occasion, at Christina's baptism. Judge Worley plans to attend.

"Congratulations, Del," the Judge greets me warmly. "I hear that you and Eli have produced a daughter."

"Yes, indeed. Quite unexpectedly, and gratefully."

He smiles with a twinkle in his eye. "I must say that you did not waste any time."

I laugh, thinking that he must have done the math. "No, sir. It actually happened immediately, though that was not something we had necessarily planned."

"Well, I think it is wonderful. And I am so glad that Sebastian got to meet her. Alberta told me how much he wanted that."

"For some reason, he especially wanted to hang on for that occasion," I comment.

"Well, that is understandable," the judge replies. I ask Judge Worley how he is doing, and he tells me that his daughter and her family have moved back to the area, and he gets to see them now much more often. I am glad for him. His daughter is a successful defense attorney in Syracuse. Some professions seem to run in families.

"She tells many tales about her clients and cases. I certainly enjoy hearing her stories. But somehow, the cases she tells me about never seen to match up with the crimes reported on the evening news," he tells me, smiling.

"You mean you think she makes up stories," I ask, amazed.

"Considering attorney privilege and her wild imagination, I think she either makes them up entirely, or perhaps collapses the details from several different cases together so I will never recognize them," he says.

"That's fascinating," I smile. He is clearly pleased that she maintains her integrity as an attorney, even if she fabricates stories for his entertainment.

As I think about Judge Worley and Sebastian, it occurs to me that I do not really know their history together. I make a mental note to ask Eli about that later. I am especially interested to know how a District Attorney and a Judge forged a personal relationship. When I do ask Eli, I am completely surprised to learn that their friendship goes back to their days as students at Yale Law School. They met one another there and were delighted to discover they both originally came from the Syracuse area, though they had not met before. Sebastian was from Chittenango, Worley from Liverpool. It is a friendship that lasted a life time.

++

There are no formal comments planned. I might have enjoyed hearing some of those, but that was not what Sebastian wanted. He wanted an informal, celebratory, hospitable gathering in his beautiful home. He would not have been disappointed. Alberta spared no detail of warmth or luxury. Hundreds of well—wishers have greeted the family.

I catch a glimpse of Eli deeply engrossed in conversation with Roger Riley. Of course, Roger would be here, because he has known the Fishers since his elementary school days. He appears to be accompanied by an attractive woman. I think they are together because of the way she touches his arm from time to time, and how he gazes at her. Eli motions for me to join them.

Roger gives me the once over and said, "Wow, Del, you look great." When I got dressed earlier in the day, I wondered whether or not my basic little black dress would fit, so I dared to try it on. It is the same dress that I wore on the first occasion when I visited Eli's home and met his parents. Eli had given me the once over that night as well, clearly impressed by what he saw. I was delighted this morning to discover that the dress fits perfectly, which means that I have recovered my pre-pregnancy body. My stomach might not be quite as flat, but still, I am quite proud of myself for what has been accomplished in three weeks' time.

"Del, this is Cassandra Cody," Roger says, introducing his guest to me. I smile at the name. It sounds a little like a Bond Girl, which is perfect for Roger Riley, James Bond himself.

"Welcome, Cassandra," I greet her. "We are glad that you could come today. It is both a sad and a happy occasion for us to remember Sebastian."

"Thank you. I've actually heard quite a lot about him," she responds. "Roger speaks of him with such respect."

"Cassandra, I think there are things about Sebastian that even Eli does not know," Roger says, mysteriously.

"Such as?" Eli asks, raising his eyebrow in surprise.

"I suppose it is no secret now, though at the time your father did not want me to tell you this. Remember when my Dad was laid off from his job right before my senior year of college?" Roger says.

"Yes, of course I remember," Eli answers.

"And you know how worried I was about being able to finish my last year?"

"As I recall, you said that your Dad got all those finances worked out, so it was no problem. I cannot recall the specific details of that time frame."

"Well, actually it was *your* father who worked out the finances. My Dad got a strange letter in the mail that summer from some attorney he did not know saying that an anonymous donor had prepaid for my senior year at Syracuse University. Dad was so relieved, he just accepted that donation as a gift from heaven. But I wanted answers. I immediately went to see Sebastian and asked him about it. At first he would not admit to it, but I wore him down. He finally told me that he liked to invest his money in young people because it was a sure bet for the future. But he said that he still wanted to be anonymous, and in particular, I was not to tell *you.* He was afraid that it might have some effect on our friendship."

The two men wander off to talk to each other privately. Eli is clearly surprised by Roger's revelation and wants to know more. In fact, many people surprise him at the reception with the stories they share about the things that Sebastian had done for them. I am anxious for Eli to share all those with me later, especially whatever he learned from Roger.

I am interested in getting to know a little bit about Cassandra. She is a beautiful blond. She is exactly the kind of beauty to whom I would have expected Roger to be attracted. But she also seems to have substance along with her beauty. I would estimate that she is in her mid to late thirties.

"Cassandra, are you a native of the Syracuse area?"

"I've lived here for the past twelve years. I play with the Syracuse Symphony," she answers. "And you can just call me Cass. It's easier."

I am impressed that she is a musician. "Thanks, Cass. What do you play?"

"I am a violinist," she says.

"Then you must know the musicians in the living room," I remark.

"Yes, all of them. In fact, had I not been coming as a guest today, I might have been playing with them. I often do."

"That is so amazing," I say, adding, "I gather that you and Roger are an item."

"I think so, though I am still trying to figure him out," she confesses. I laugh. So am I, for that matter. Roger is a most intriguing person, smart, charismatic, and handsome. But at least for me, it is always difficult to tell whether he is teasing or serious. He puts one off their guard.

"How long have you been seeing each other?" I ask.

"For the past six months, and he has definitely been the pursuer. I know Roger has been married before, so I have not been expecting much out of this relationship. In fact, at first, he told me had sworn off of marriage."

"And do you think that has changed?"

"I don't know for sure, but he is moving pretty fast, and being very romantic," she reveals. If Roger is really interested in a woman, I would imagine that he would indeed be a romantic. "He told me a little about you and Eli, and he said that Eli didn't waste any time marrying you."

I laugh. "That's true."

But of course, I know that there is a lot more to the story than that. We met and had been attracted to one another. He helped me uncover my history, thanks to Roger's help, and in the process we fell in love. The signs that we belong together were so strong that we were completely stunned, and unable to ignore them. It still sounds quite odd to think about reading the signs. But I do think that people do that.

"And I understand that now you have a little girl."

"Yes, her name is Christina, and she is definitely a joy."

"Roger said that you gave birth at forty-one, if you don't mind my mentioning that."

"No, I don't mind. I am certainly both blessed and proud. Do you mind me asking if you have been married before, or had children?"

"No to both of those questions. I would certainly love to have a child, though I don't feel any sense of urgency about it. I probably should, since I am thirty seven and the old biological clock is ticking."

"Maybe that is why Roger is moving fast."

"Somehow I don't think so. He has never even mentioned a desire for children, but you never know."

We see the two men are coming toward us again, each with a glass of wine in both hands, presumably two of them are for each of us. Cass and I take the glasses gratefully. I notice that Roger has brought a red wine for her, and I am a white wine drinker.

Roger says, "Del, Eli tells me that you are thinking about selling your house."

"Yes, we have been talking about it, but it is not on the market yet," I respond.

"Just for the record, I am interested in buying that house."

I could not contain my surprise, "You are? Have you even seen it Roger?"

"Yes, I saw it once last year, when I brought a box of paperwork along for you to look at."

"Oh, yes. I do recall that."

"I especially love the location and the privacy. It isn't part of a suburban development, and I like that. It also has a lot of potential. As I recall, you only used a portion of the house."

"Yes, that's true."

"Well, I can picture all kinds of possibilities there. So maybe when you are really serious about selling, you'll let me know."

Nothing could have surprised me more. And I do like the idea of selling my house to someone I know. I wonder what Cassandra thinks about this conversation.

I learn later that evening from Eli that it is really Cassandra who had fallen in love with the location and the cottage. They had been out driving in that vicinity one day, and Roger just spontaneously decided to drive into the place to show her. It strikes me as too small for them, but maybe as a starter house, it will be just perfect. And Roger is right; there is plenty of room to expand with endless possibilities.

I see Nanny coming toward me, carrying Christina. Her given name is Nancy. Not surprisingly, a Nanny nickname stuck. It is not only what she does, but what she is called.

I am glad that I will be able to show Christina off to both Roger and Cass. She is a beautiful child with a pleasant demeanor. So far, she has also been an easy child. After the first two weeks, she started sleeping through most of the night, waking for an early morning feeding, and then going back to sleep.

I do hope that since she is such an easy baby that will not mean she will be difficult later.

CHAPTER 21

CHRISTINA'S BAPTISM

I am so glad that my Dad and my brother and his family are coming for the day. I do not get to see them as often as I should. Eli and I have gone there to the farm in Newark Valley to visit them twice this year. They rarely travel because they are so tied down to the milking. This will actually be the first time my whole family has been to our home in Chittenango. I am not sure that I have prepared them for the size and elegance of our house. I am not sure I have completely acclimated to it myself. Our lives are so different from theirs, from my childhood. I know that my family will be gracious, and happy for me, but also surprised.

We are all scheduled to meet at the Community Church for the eleven o'clock service, and then we will come back here for a family meal in the dining room. Alberta has even made arrangements with the caterer from Sebastian's reception to prepare most of Sunday's meal as well. We just have to put it in the oven and do the finishing touches.

I ask Eli about the baptismal service and what to expect. He told me that he will invite all family members to stand with us. That would include Alberta, of course, as well as my father Frank, and my brother Frank, Junior, along with Linda and their children.

I do not have any specific christening gown for Christina to wear. Alberta said that she knew that Sebastian had been baptized in the Catholic Church, but she does not have any mementoes of that occasion. I purchased a simple white dress on-line for the occasion. I do wish that we had something of more sentimental value, but I could never in a million years have anticipated what actually happened.

Last year, Roger and I made a trip to Rome and I met Cardinal Conti. He is my biological father. My birth is the result of a love affair he had with my mother Iris when he was a young man before he entered the priesthood. At that meeting, Both Roger and I were stunned that he did not try to deny his paternity when I confronted him. What was even more surprising was that he said he was going to tell his mother this news, and that she would be thrilled. Mother Crechea, as he called her, was eighty seven years old at that time. Cardinal Conti and I have shared several correspondences since last year, and he knows of my marriage and pregnancy. His full name is Philippe Domenico Crechea Conti. Whenever I think of him, I tend to think of him as *The Cardinal*, with a capital *T,* both to signify his rank and his significance in my life. It is strange to think that my biological mother Iris Pope just thought of him as Nico. Clearly, she did not think of him as a priest.

Cardinal Conti's Mother Crechea sent us a package, which we received a week before the time of Christina's baptism. Inside was a hand written note, along with the most exquisite infant baptismal gown I have ever seen. It is a cream colored satin gown with tiny pearls hand sewn into the fabric.

Mother Crechea wrote:

> *My dear grand-daughter*
> *Delight Crechea,*
>
> *Nothing would give this old heart greater pleasure than for your daughter, my great-granddaughter Christina, to wear this gown at her baptism. I have no other use for it, as I do not expect any other children or grandchildren to enter my life at this point. Please keep it in your family. This garment was worn by my son Philippe Conti on the occasion of his baptism at the Church of San Domenico Maggiore in Naples, Italy. May your child be as much of a blessing to you and to the world as mine has been to me.*
>
> *Sophia Crechea*

++

As we approach the church, I appreciate the beauty of the day. The autumn colors are at their peak, and the sun is shining and the sky is a brilliant blue. Dad and Junior and his family are waiting for me in the foyer of the church. We all embrace and greet one another with affection. My Dad seems especially relaxed and beaming. It is so good to see that. He has struggled so much with his grief since my mother's death. The church is filled with people on this particular Sunday. We are ushered to the front two rows, reserved for the occasion of baptism on this day. Eli has not yet entered the sanctuary. I know that he first prays with the choir, and then spends a few moments centering himself and preparing his spirit. I cannot even imagine what he must be feeling today. I know that I am feeling a sense of awe.

Christina is awake. I am grateful that she is such an easy-going and placid child. Eli and I have often commented that this cannot be what most parents experience. We have not had to deal with colic, nor fussiness. We have been very grateful that she even got into a rhythm of sleeping through the nights early in her life. We could not be more fortunate, as far as a baby's temperament.

As we stand and sing the first hymn, I place Christina on my shoulder, and she smiles at the people behind us. They are delighted by her smiles. Dad holds the hymnal so I have both hands free for the baby.

I have become much better acquainted with many members of the congregation over the months of my pregnancy. They have been interested and curious about us and our lives, but not pushy or intrusive. I do know that it helps a great deal that we live in our own home, rather than in a house next door to the church. This church has never actually had a home directly on the church premises. They did own one in a neighborhood. When Eli came, they voted to sell the manse they did use, and if necessary in the future, to buy another one in another neighborhood.

Since we live a few miles away in Chittenango, and since I became pregnant, I have not felt the pressure to attend every function, every time the church doors are open. Eli tells me that sometimes pastor's wives have to deal with those expectations. Eli has clearly wanted to protect me from many of those challenges. I assume he has heard of these concerns from other pastors, since he has not had a family of his own before now.

I am sure the time will come when I will want to be more involved in the parts of the ministry that interest me the most. I certainly would love to learn more about the bible, and in fact, I would even some day hope to lead a discussion class. There are various small groups at this church, and those are certainly not all led by the pastor. Before I would teach such a class, I have decided that I want to take some courses so that I have enough confidence. But all of that will unfold in its time.

Eli is now speaking about the meaning and significance of baptism, and its history. He takes a silver pitcher off of the chancel table and walks over to the baptismal font. I can see that soon our child will be baptized by her father. She is wearing the gown worn by my father, Cardinal Conti, on the occasion of his baptism. Soon we are all invited to stand around the font. Eli holds the silver pitcher about twelve inches above the marble font and pours the water in. You can hear the sound it makes. I feel chills run up my arms. So much has happened to bring us to this moment. It is almost as if Eli has read my mind, because he says almost those exact words.

"So much has happened to bring us to this point. In the beginning, God's spirit swept across the deep, and out of the chaos brought forth light and life. In time, a child was nurtured in the water of his mother's womb. Jesus was baptized by John and anointed by God's own spirit. He calls us all to share in this baptism."

Now I feel the chills creeping up my back. I also think that I hear sounds coming from the back of the sanctuary. It sounds like a movement of air. I dare not turn around. I do see a surprised look on Eli's face, or maybe it is a look of wonder. I notice that there is movement in Christina's gown at the bottom, even though Eli now holds her motionless. Am I imagining this? Were others aware of what I was either imaging or experiencing? Our backs are to the congregation, so I cannot tell. Suddenly, I feel Alberta's hand touch mine and squeeze it. That is so unexpected that it confirms to me that she is experiencing something unusual herself. Perhaps she feels Sebastian's presence. I like thinking he is right here with us.

Eli said the prayer of thanksgiving over the water. He places one of his hands inside the water in the baptismal font. That is when I see a tear stream down his face. The sound of the air moving has intensified. There is no murmur coming from the congregation, so I assume they are unaware of it. There is total silence. It is a silence of wonder.

"Pour out your Holy Spirit on this water and bless the one who receives it, and bless us all, for it is in our dying that we are raised with Christ, that we share in the final victory. All glory and honor is yours, Almighty God, now and forever."

Eli held Christina's head over the font, cradling her with the crook of his arm. It struck me that this is something he has done many times before. But never like this, with his own child. She looks up and smiles at him as if she is a hundred years old, and understands everything that is happening.

With a seashell in his other hand, Eli pours water over her head. She makes no protest, as if she senses the solemnity of the moment.

"In the name of the Father." Now Christina grabs her father's thumb which is wrapped around her.

"And of the Son." I look at my Dad, who is clearly moved, as I am myself.

"And of the Holy Spirit. Amen." Tears stream down both of Eli's cheeks now.

For me at least, the sound of the wind in the sanctuary is now unmistakable. I have heard it before. Most recently, I had such an experience at my grandmother Grace's memorial site.

They are the winds of the spirit. I know they speak their presence this day. I hear them say: *You are my beloved child.*

Christina.

CHAPTER 22

SEPTEMBER 2009
FRANK WILLIAMS

I am headed to visit my Dad today in Newark Valley. It has almost been a year since the occasion of Christina's baptism. It was the strangest thing. When we all got back to our house for lunch that day, no one spoke about the unusual things that had occurred during the service. We went about our lunch as if nothing had happened, but I know better.

Eli and I discussed the significance of that event for weeks afterward. He also felt the winds of the spirit blowing in that place. Other than that, neither of us really understood exactly what had happened. Were we the only ones who felt and heard it? Eventually, we stopped talking about it altogether. I think in time we probably convinced ourselves that we had imagined most of it, or created it in our own minds. That is understandable, since any suggestion of supernatural occurrences is too irrational to give serious consideration.

Christina is staying at home today keeping Alberta company. Christina is and always has been a delightful child, full of laughter and joy. At one year old, she speaks in phrases; two or three word sentences often come out of her mouth. She loves learning new words, and she picks them up so quickly, like a sponge. She has dark wavy hair, even darker than either Eli's or mine, and she also has brown eyes that sparkle. She is walking now, so that creates a new set of challenges for us. We have learned how to baby-proof a house.

Today, I want a chance to visit with my Dad and find out what is going on in his life. He greets me warmly, and he is clearly happy to see me.

"Welcome, Del. It's so good to see you!"

"Hi, Dad." I give him a big hug. I try to go and visit every three months. "You look great! So fill me in on what is happening with you."

We find ourselves sitting at the kitchen table. I remember the many months of Dad's silence and depression and am so glad that seems to be behind him.

"Del, I want you to know that I am planning to make some major changes in my life," he announces.

"Meaning you are going to retire?" Even though he is well beyond retirement age, I never really thought that he would.

"How did you guess?" he asks.

"That's the biggest thing I can think of," I answer.

"I am still in good health, so I have decided that now I am going to enjoy my last days."

"Good for you, Dad, I'm so glad to hear that! So tell me about your plans."

"I'm turning everything over to Junior and I'm going to walk away completely," he says.

"That's hard to imagine."

"Well, it's past time. I don't want to be one of those farmers who is never able to retire. And the business is changing so much all of the time. Junior is great at keeping up with all the technology as well as the agricultural theory. But I just don't have the heart for it anymore."

"Have you given any thought to how you will spend your time?"

"First, I am going to buy a little house in town, and get myself set up there."

"A townie?" I tease. "Will miracles never cease?"

"I don't want to be under foot for Frank Junior. For the first year, I plan to do some traveling. I think I'll take one of those Viking River Tours. Then when I get that out of my system, I might go into politics."

"Politics? What do you mean?"

"I think I'd like to run for the school board."

"Oh, you'd be really good at that, Dad." Dad had always been involved with the school in one way or another, as a coach, as a member of the parents' association.

"And then after that, I might run for mayor."

"Does Newark Valley even have a major?"

"Of course they do. And if that goes well, I might even run for the state assembly."

"You are certainly ambitious all of a sudden. I'm proud of you!" And even though I am surprised by these revelations, I am truly proud. It is as if my Dad suddenly has a new lease on life.

"So what about you, Del?" he asks.

"What do you mean?" I ask.

"Do you have any specific plans?"

"You mean, for my life?" I ask.

"Yes."

"Well, I'm going to raise Christina," I say.

"And that is a wonderful and noble thing," Dad says. "From where I sit, Del, it looks to me like you could do just about anything you want to do. You'd have family support, and obviously enough resources. She's as easy a child as I've ever seen, and you could have lots of help with her."

"Well, I have thought about taking some courses at seminary."

"Good. I think you should," he affirms.

It isn't like my Dad to be pushing me. It does bring back memories of my mother suggesting that once I find out the truth about my past, it might lead me toward a different future. So far, that has definitely proven to be true.

"And, by the way, Del, you might want to know that your Aunt Sandy is failing these days. Her mind is still sharp, but apparently she has some form of leukemia and her days are numbered."

"I'm so sorry to hear that, Dad."

"You really ought to go and see her, you know."

"Yes, I should," I agree. She has played such a key role in my life. I cannot imagine what might have happened to me if she had not been friends with my grandmother Grace. If Sandy had not brought me to Frank and Ida in Newark Valley, maybe I would have become a ward of the state and gone into the system down there in Mississippi. I suppose that could not have been any worse than what my great-grandmother Deborah went through living at Willard for twenty years. But I am grateful that New York is my home.

I still think of her occasionally, and I especially remember going to the exhibit at the Everson Museum. I even remember the exact date, April 21, 2007. That would be almost two and a half years ago now. Sometimes that feels like yesterday, and at other times it seems like a hundred years ago. By any estimation, it was a defining moment in my life, for it sent me on a journey of self-discovery. Of course, I am still on that journey. Dad's remarks are a stark reminder of that. At the very least, I take those to mean that I cannot rest on my laurels, but must continue to grow and learn. I suspect that raising Christina will require my constantly being on my toes. I can tell already that she is an inquisitive one.

+++

Since I have a free day, I decide to go from my Dad's house to Aunt Sandy's assisted living facility in Binghamton. It is as lovely as I remember it, and there is the same sign on the same door. Sandra Bradford. I knock. I knock a second time, somewhat louder.

"Come in," a voice says.

"Hello, Aunt Sandy," I greet, going to where she is in her comfortable chaise lounge type chair, which is adjustable to numerous positions, not unlike a hospital bed. This is new since I last saw her.

"So it looks like my long lost niece, Del," Sandy says.

"Yes, it's me."

"Well, I'm always glad to see you, dear," Sandy says. She seems to have mellowed somewhat since I last saw her.

"What brings you here today?" she asks.

"Dad said you are having some health issues, so I wanted to drop by just to say hello," I explain.

"Good-bye, you mean," she remarks, sounding more like the Sandy I remember, outspoken and to the point.

"Well, I hope not," I answer.

"I don't expect it to be too long now," she says.

"I'm so sorry to hear that, Sandy."

"Don't be."

"I was thinking when I was driving over here that I have so much to thank you for," I comment.

"Such as," she asks.

"Oh, you know, for saving my life," I answer.

"I did what she asked me to because I owed Grace more than you could ever know," Sandy says. My grandmother asked Sandy to take care of me, should anything happen to her, and of course, it did.

"Maybe I saved your life. Who knows? I like to think you have had a better life here." You probably would have survived if I'd left you there. But I couldn't do that."

"Why not?" I ask.

"Because she saved my soul."

"Wow," I answer, surprised by this news, or at least surprised to hear those words coming from Sandy.

"She never knew that. But she inspired me to be a better person. And after her death, and after I dropped you off with Frank and Ida and went to California, I became a different person. Before that, before I knew her, I was sleeping around wherever I could," Sandy confesses.

"I do have a few memories of Granny Grace now," I say.

"Well, you're lucky if you do," she comments.

"Strangely enough, most of them are from when she was preaching," I confess.

"And why do you find that strange?" Sandy asks.

"Oh, I don't know. You'd think they would be more grandmotherly memories, rather than preacher memories. Did you ever hear her preach, Sandy?" I wonder.

"Just once," she says. "It was the Sunday before her death. For some reason, I was afraid to go inside the church. I thought my husband would kill me if he heard about it. People were very upset about an integrated church."

"So, what did you do?"

"I stood outside the window and listened. I'd never heard words like hers before. They were such simple words, but so profound. I have heard some preachers in Newark Valley, and the stuff they said was complete nonsense, quoting different scholars and theologians. People slept through most of it. Grace just told stories. And every story she told was connected with the scripture she read. It's hard to describe. But on that day, standing outside that church, listening through the open window, I knew that I had just been introduced to the Creator, no doubt about it. And I vowed to be a better person."

"I'm so glad you told me that, Sandy. It helps me to understand both of you so much better."

"I hear you've had a little girl."

"Yes, she is a special little girl."

"Grace would have really loved her," Sandy says.

"I know."

"Ida, too," she adds.

"Yes, especially Ida," I smile, thinking of my adoptive mother.

For some reason, completely out of the blue, I think of the story of Ruth and Naomi. Naomi, the mother-in-law, became more like Ruth's mother. Ruth was from Moab, a foreign land to Naomi. Eli always said that story reminds him of me. I can see some of the parallels. From Ruth's marriage to Boaz, a son was born. From my marriage to Eli, a daughter is born. And we have named her Ruth. Eli sees many other similarities as well.

When I chose that name for Supreme Court reasons, I had not even thought of the biblical Ruth. Eli made that connection immediately.

Ruth and Naomi returned from the land of Moab to Bethlehem of Judea.

I decide that I need to go back and read that story again. There must be something I am missing.

CHAPTER 23

ALBERTA 2010

Since Christina was born two years ago, ninety year old Alberta Fisher has been an amazing, energetic grandmother. Sometimes I thought that she had more energy than I had. It has been a good thing that we have had this time to spend time together—Alberta, Eli, Christina, and me. Last night Alberta died peacefully in her sleep. Thankfully, it was Eli who found her this morning. When she did not appear in the kitchen after a while, he went to her room. It was likely either a heart attack or a stroke. She had no other illness of which we were aware.

Christina adores her grandmother, so I cannot imagine how we will explain death to her at only two years old. I think I will leave that to Eli, who will surely do a better job at describing heaven than I can. I do definitely believe that there is a heaven. I choose to also believe that Alberta will be there waiting for us when it is our turn. It could not be heaven otherwise. A better mother-in-law a daughter-in-law could not have imagined.

Both of Eli's parents have been wonderful to me, patient, and best of all, never judgmental. When I first met Eli's family, I was a mess, at least emotionally, having just confronted my own mother's death, and the strange lockbox papers she left for me. For a long time after that, I was confused and did not know exactly how to move forward with my life. That's when I found myself pulling into the parking lot of the Jamesville Community Church one Sunday morning. How does one understand such an out of character action? I attended church occasionally with my family in Newark Valley, but had not done so during all my years in Syracuse. And yet, there I was.

Over time, I have learned to be grateful for all of those family secrets—the ones about my birth parents, and my grandmother Grace's death, the story of Aunt Sandy bringing me to New York. All of those events led me to where I am today, and to Eli and to Christina. How hard it is for me to imagine a life without either of them. I smile now to think of what an independent soul I was before meeting Eli. I still have tendencies toward being independent, wanting my own identity. There is nothing keeping me from any of that. Eli has always been open and encouraging with me, no matter what. At the moment, I am enjoying an interdependent family dynamic. I do find that preferable to my former solitary life.

Alberta had insisted that we save Sebastian's ashes and not scatter them as he had directed. She wants both of their ashes to be scattered at the same time. None of us thought that he would mind, so we have waited, as she asked. Alberta has been very specific about what she wished to happen when she died. Alberta sat us down shortly after Sebastian's reception and gave us directions for her own similar event, only much more low key. That was when she told us to keep his ashes and to scatter them both together, making sure that some of his and her ashes end up sharing some the same places, not at separate locations on the property.

Christina came bouncing into the kitchen, still dressed in her pajamas, her feet bare. She had beautiful dark brown eyes, and shoulder length brown wavy hair. She is such a happy child. Every time I notice the bottom of her right foot, I am somewhat mystified. The birthmark which was more of a blob when she was born, is clearly changing. From a rather amorphous plus-sign shape, the edges have become more defined. I think that is especially strange, that a birthmark should change. After all, a birthmark is there at birth. I would expect such a mark to be unchanging. But I do clearly see changes in Christina's.

Eli does not seemed to notice, nor to be concerned, so I have only mentioned it once or twice. The best way that I can describe the changes is to say that each of the four ends of the plus sign now have curling, split edges. This morning the whole mark appears to be a much brighter red than usual.

Christina can tell by the feeling in the room that things are not the same. She is very intuitive.

"Where's Nanna?" she asks immediately.

Eli and I look at one another. He can tell that I want him to handle this conversation. He lifts Chrissy into his lap. She sits with a serious little face, waiting, sensing. She seems always able to read the emotions of those around her.

"What's wrong, Daddy?" Christina asks, putting her hand gently on his cheek.

"Your Nanna won't be coming for breakfast this morning," Eli explains.

"Is she sick?" Chrissy asks.

"No, honey. She won't be coming back at all. Her body is still here, but her spirit has left."

"Oh," she nods, as if she understands. "Don't worry Daddy; Granddaddy is waiting for her there."

I saw the tear move slowly down Eli's cheek and the little child reached up and kissed the place where the tear had been. Christina herself did not cry. She seems to know exactly what has happened. So often, she has been a difficult child to comprehend. One moment she giggles and plays exactly like every other child her age, and the next moment, she sounds like a wise old soul. I never know exactly what to make of it. When she said Granddaddy is waiting, I realize that she has made an instant connection between Sebastian and Alberta both being in heaven. We have often said that Granddaddy is in heaven. Christina does not remember her grandfather Sebastian, since he died the day after she was born.

"Will I see Nanna again, Daddy?" she asks.

"Not any time soon, Chrissy," Eli said. "But yes, someday, for sure. If you love someone, they are always with you. You'll see them again. I think heaven is a big happy reunion of people who love one another."

"Can we have a reunion for Nanna now?" she asks.

"That's exactly what we are going to do, Chrissy. We're going to have a big party and invite all Nanna's friends," Eli says.

"Oh, goodie," she says, sounding like any two year old, perhaps imagining balloons and cake.

In fact, Alberta had said she wanted a similar event to the one we had for Sebastian, though more festive, less formal and on a much smaller scale. She insisted that she had not left the same kind of legacy that he had. Alberta's legacy is significant, having made her mark in environmental conservation. She must have taught hundreds and hundreds of students over the course of her career at State University of New York at Syracuse.

In the days that followed, we made plans for a party for Alberta. We followed the model she had used for Sebastian, only this time, Eli said that he was going to make remarks and give others the opportunity to share any memories they might have. We contacted the same caterer. Eli and I went through family pictures. There was a whole chest full of them. Unfortunately, many of the older photographs were not marked in any way, and even Eli did not know who they were. I wished that we had spent the time to ask Alberta about the pictures, but that was not something we thought to do.

++

Since both of his parents have now passed on, Eli is the executor of both his parents' estates, and the heir to their wealth. Eli told me that Alberta had left many generous donations to local charities, from the Rescue Mission, to the Salvation Army, to Hospice. I was more than stunned to learn that Alberta had left half a million dollars, specifically to me. I did not understand that.

"Eli, did you know about this?" I ask.

"Yes, she told me," he admits.

"But why in the world would she do that?" I ask Eli.

"My mother was an independent woman and she very much believed that every woman should have money in her own name, not just jointly with her husband. She wanted you to have something that was just yours," he explains.

"But what in the world will I do with it?"

"Whatever you might wish," he adds, not at all surprised or concerned. Eli had grown up with wealth and has always been nonchalant about finances. I come from a farm where money to spend varies wildly from year to year. Two bad years in a row demanded significant sacrifices.

I already do have some funds in my own name, from the sale of my house to Roger Riley. Over the years that I lived in my cottage house, I often paid double on my mortgage payments, so there was very little left on the mortgage by the time I sold it. The revenue from the sale of my house provides more money in the bank than I ever expected to see in my name.

This additional money from Alberta will now really challenge me to consider all the ways that I can do good. I will find ministries to support, and charities. I decide then and there that I will devise a giving plan, which will include both local agencies and charities, as well as others on a more global scale. For sure, I want to give a significant gift to Vera House, a shelter for victims of domestic abuse. Thinking about how to manage this money wisely leads me to conclude that life is much simpler without it.

+

Roger is currently in the middle of remodeling the carriage house cottage and adding to it. It is obvious that he plans to marry Cassandra Cody, and this is his gift to her. Three years ago I could not have imagined Roger getting to this point, but he does seem happy. I do wish them both well, and look forward to seeing them at Alberta's party, as we have begun to call it.

Thinking about the wealth that Eli will oversee, makes me think about his church, and how it is financed. Now that I have been through several cycles of the church year there, I do know that once a year there is a Stewardship Focus, and the members are asked to make a financial commitment.

Eli himself never seems to mention that particular aspect of his ministry. Once I asked him about it. He explained to me how he felt.

"I am in an especially unique position, Del, as far as funding the ministry of the church goes," he begins. "I've always known that my family has money, so I've never needed to feel any concern about the church budget."

"You mean, about your salary," I ask.

"Well, yes, certainly that. I know that other pastors do have to worry about the funds because their livelihood depends upon it. But I'm not in the ministry because I have to make a living out of it."

"I can see how that would certainly be a benefit," I acknowledge.

"And the amazing thing is, because I am free from those concerns, there has never been a year of ministry in my life where finances for the church came up short. It all takes care of itself, just as it should."

"Not even back in Seattle, when you first started a church?"

"No, not even then. There were several families who met together and decided that they would provide my salary for the first five years, and after that I would be on my own."

"How did that work out?" I ask.

"After the first four years, we had a building and enough people to pay for the ministry. Then after twelve years, we had to build a much larger facility," Eli shares.

"I guess it would be accurate to say that you are not in the ministry because of the money," I tease.

"To tell you the truth, I made a deal with God," Eli confesses.

"You did?" I am surprised. I didn't think you were supposed to make deals with God. And you are probably not supposed to look for signs either.

"Yes. I promised that I would give everything. My talent, my energy, my full commitment, my dedication, if in return, God would take care of the financial side of ministry.

"And that has worked, I gather."

"Yes, always."

++

Alberta's Party was just exactly what she would have wanted. By the time one is ninety years old, many friends and acquaintances have already passed on. Still, there were a significant number of people who came to honor her memory—some from the faculty at SUNY Environmental Science and Forestry where she had worked, some from charities she had supported, or women's groups in which she had participated. Others were friends of Sebastian's, or friends of ours. A steady flow of folks cycled through the Fisher estate.

Rather than providing photo boards, at her request, we had one lovely floral arrangement in each room of the house. They were not funeral style arrangements, but arrangements in vases both large and small. Each arrangement matched the color scheme of the room. That had also been Alberta's idea.

I am happy to see Roger Riley and Cassandra Cody. They are obviously a serious couple now. Eli and I have been out to dinner with them occasionally, but mostly we prefer to spend our evenings at home with Christina and each other.

"Del," Roger greets me, "Boy do I have news for you!" He gives me a quick hug.

I am not expecting any news from Roger, so this greeting takes me by surprise. I also gave Cass a warm greeting. Eli is in another room greeting the guests.

"What news?" I ask, truly puzzled.

"You might want to be sitting down for this one," he warns.

I could not in my wildest dreams imagine what Roger could possibly have to tell me. He knows that Eli and I had made the trip to Indianola to see my grandmother's monument, and that pleased him. But I feel like I have already received all the family information that he could possibly pass along.

Roger takes my elbow and leads me to a more private corner of the room.

"Do you remember Carolyn Wilson?" he asks. The name does sound familiar, but I cannot make an immediate connection.

"Carolyn Wilson, nee Carolyn Oliver, from Ovid, New York, daughter of Hoss Oliver, friend of Dalton Duncan," Roger rattles off.

"Oh yes, the woman who ended up with Deborah White's journal." It did not take me long to piece it together.

"One and the same," Roger confirms.

"So what's the news?" I ask.

"It turns out that our little Carolyn from Seneca County is quite a resourceful woman. Or at least, one with all the right connections and a lot of luck. Believe it or not, she has a first cousin who lives in Los Angeles." I wait for him to go on.

"So?"

"And this first cousin just happens to be a successful screenwriter," Roger says.

"A screenwriter?" I repeat, wondering for a moment exactly what a screenwriter does.

"Carolyn Oliver sent her the journal. She turned it into a movie." Even unflappable Roger seems stunned by this turn of events.

"You've got to be kidding!"

"I'm not kidding. In fact, the movie is due to be released next year. Big names, too. Kathryn Bigelow is directing."

"Didn't she just win an Oscar a couple of months ago," I say, my jaw literally dropping.

"Yes, for *The Foot Locker*," Roger acknowledges. "The new one is just being called *Willard.*"

"How did you find out about this?"

"It just fell into my lap. This is one thing that I didn't ferret out myself, at least not at first," Roger confesses. "I overheard two attorneys talking in a restaurant downtown. One mentioned the making of a movie about Willard. I got up and went over to their table and told them I have a client in Ovid who worked at Willard until it closed in 1995. I said she would be really interested to know about the movie."

"You just made that up, right?" I ask.

"Yeah, pretty much, but after I heard the rumor from them, I went to Ovid myself to check it out. Sure enough, there had been a filming crew around the old Psychiatric facility for several months of last year."

I try to wrap my mind around this bit of amazing news, but it is really hard to imagine. Then I think to ask, "So who is playing Deborah White?"

"I hear there are three actor—one for her childhood, and another one for her youth. The adult version of Deborah is played by Helen Hunt," Roger says.

"Well, I'm happy about that, at least." She is an actor I admire. And what about Dalton?

"Same story—three actors. The adult Dalton is Hugh Jackman," he adds.

I laughed at this bit of news. I'm a big fan. "I'm even happier about that."

"So how do you feel about this movie, Del?" Roger asks.

"I have no idea," I admit honestly. "Did you say when it is due out?"

"Next fall 2011," he answers. "I think I read that it has a September release date."

++

I will have to think long and hard about whether or not I really want to see the movie. After learning about my great-grandmother's years at Willard, I had plenty of nightmares just imagining it.

Then it occurs to me that Carolyn Wilson, who has the journal, would have information and insight from the horse's own mouth, so to speak. How much do I really want to know? And how much of the movie would be accurate and how much fabricated? At the moment I am not at all sure how I felt about this new wrinkle.

I wait until later in the evening, after Christina is asleep, and Eli and I are alone in our bedroom, to break the news to him of the upcoming movie.

He thinks it will be interesting to see the characters brought to life. After discussing it for quite a while, we both agree that the stories of these peoples' lives deserve to be told. First, as patients, they were hidden away at the asylum; then their stories were hidden away for years in suitcases found in the attic at the state hospital.

Deborah White's journal was tucked away in the attic of her old house in Ovid. It did almost seem like she wanted to be heard, to have her say, to tell her story.

Still, I do wonder how Deborah might feel about her story being made into a movie, putting her life and her thoughts out there on the screen for the world to see and hear and experience.

I decide that since so much time has passed since her death, maybe it can no longer be considered a personal intrusion. I can well imagine that the movie *Willard* will be a compelling movie indeed.

I am just not sure if I can bear to see it.

CHAPTER 24

THE INCIDENT, SUMMER 2011

What a glorious June day it is. The sun is shining; the sky is a clear and beautiful blue. For some reason, it reminds me of the same kind of beautiful day almost ten years ago when the world became a different world after the September terrorist attacks. The loveliness of that day was so incongruous with the ugliness of all that happened. I remember admiring what a lovely day it was on the way to work. Then the world changed just a little later that morning. How strange to think about ten years ago, and what a different person I was then.

My friend from church, Allison, has invited me and Christina for a play date at Green Lakes State Park. We will meet at the playground there. Allison's daughter Andrea is a few months older than Christina. She turned three last month, and Christina has a September birthday. Allison and I struck up a friendship when I led a bible study on the Beatitudes earlier in the year. I have more confidence in myself as a teacher now, since I have taken two courses at

Colgate Rochester Crozer Divinity School, most recently a New Testament course. I remember when I first found my way there. The setting is awe-inspiring, aptly called "The Hill" with lovely views overlooking the city. The seminary is surrounded by a fence and has a pillared gate entrance.

The first time that I drove to the campus I just wanted to explore my options for taking courses and look around. I drove the Thruway from Syracuse to Rochester, taking Route 490 into Rochester; then I got off the interstate onto Goodman Street. It was a short distance from the highway exit to the campus entrance, perhaps no more than a mile or two. But how striking was the distance from the urban reality of dangerous streets, to the isolated cocoon on the hillside. I literally drove through the gates into a different world, one which felt so foreign to me at first.

The daily chapel worship was an enlightening experience for me, as the worship is led by students from various backgrounds and traditions. The experiences of Black Church worship were the most thrilling. Their tradition of call and response is so different from anything I have ever known. The congregation responds verbally to what the preacher says. "Amen. Preach it. Go on, now. Uh-huh." It has a musical cadence, as if both the preacher and the listeners know the tune. In a way, I suppose they do.

Like the man without a country, I am still the woman without a tradition. The church that my family attended in Newark Valley is a United Methodist Church, but I am not familiar enough with the history and policies of that denomination to claim it as my own. And now I attend a non-denominational Community Church where Eli is the pastor.

Allison Wood joined our church a year ago. Like me, she only has one child, though she is at least five years younger than I am. She has told me that she still hopes they will be able to have another child. It has been interesting for us both to see how Andrea and Christina have become friends. One would not expect a young child to have clear preferences in their relationships, but indeed they do seem drawn to one child more than another. Christina lights up whenever she sees Andrea at church. They also enjoy one another's company in the nursery during worship. First Eli gives the children a message, and then they are dismissed during a hymn and adjourn to their own room.

Allison and I have shared our birth experiences, perhaps like soldiers share their war stories. My story of Christina's birth is always entertaining. Allison laughs a lot, trying to picture Eli delivering a baby at night, with a lantern shining from his forehead. Allison's birth experience was also dramatic, but far scarier. She was in hard labor for over twenty four hours, and several times, the baby was in distress. Allison was determined not to have a C-section, and wanted to wait it out. Finally the baby was born, but Allison says that even after five years, she still hasn't forgotten the pain. In the back of my mind, I wonder whether that might be a deterrent to another pregnancy. I think that the mind and the body are mysterious entities, not always perfectly aligned.

I have assembled a small bag of snacks, both for the little girls, and for the bigger girls, grapes and graham crackers for them, and strawberries and chocolate cookies for us. Christina is a very precocious child, not only with advanced language skills far beyond her years, but also with a kind of mature wisdom that marks her nature. These are not just the words of a proud mother, but also the comments of others who have observed her. I have often attributed it to the fact that she has been raised by older adults, older parents and a devoted grandmother. Except for her church activities and friends, Christina has not yet encountered a large number of children her own age. We have a nanny on call for those times when neither Eli nor I can be at home to take care of our daughter.

Last year, when she was two, I was gone two days a week taking my seminary course, and Nanny stayed with her then. Nanny came into our lives when Sebastian first got sick, and she has been like a family member since that time. While younger than Alberta by at least twenty years, they still became dear friends. Proximity and need will sometimes forge deep friendships. Nanny has tended to all members of the Fisher family in various ways at one time or another, from Sebastian all the way down to Christina.

Although Eli has never been debilitated, he has let Nanny fix his breakfast on occasion, while she was bustling around the kitchen for other people. Being a caregiver is Nanny's natural calling in life. And fortunate are those who have benefitted from it. If she is taking care of Christina, I never have to worry about either one of them.

Leading a church is clearly Eli's calling. Once again, he has been quite successful at the Jamesville Church. Now he is in demand in other venues as well, serving on different boards and agencies in the greater Syracuse area. He does have to be careful not to take on too much. Just keeping up with his own flock is a significant challenge, particularly when it comes to hospital visits. There are four different hospitals where his presence might be needed—St. Joe's, Crouse, University, and Community General. With a congregation the size that Eli's now is, the demand for funerals and weddings and baptisms is sometimes daunting. Each one takes preparation time for Eli. He makes sure that he personalizes each situation with his comments, and that requires meeting with the individuals involved.

I have always found it a little strange that Eli actually enjoys doing funerals. There are many occasions where a well-known individual will draw a large crowd, and fill up the sanctuary. He told me that he feels more of an urgency to honor those with more humble endings, where there are likely to be only a few family or friends present. I have learned in the past couple of years that often more people show up for the calling hours to greet the family, rather than to the service itself. That strikes me as odd, but I suppose that is about showing respect to the living more than to the deceased. Eli focuses on the latter.

I will confess that I continue to be surprised by how demanding Eli's work is. He goes into his office six mornings a week, including Saturday, which he says is his Sabbath time. Friday is his day off and he protects that fiercely. If he has evening meetings, he does make a point to take equivalent afternoon time off from work. Eli is extremely hard working and dedicated. Because people can see that, they respond with their own commitments, both in time and money.

++

Christina and Andrea laugh and giggle as they embrace one another in greeting. Then they are off to play together. I notice again that the weather is perfect. One wants to take notice of that when it happens, because it is a rare occasion in central New York where the swings in temperature and weather can be extreme and rapid. That is especially true in Syracuse, which frequently has the honor of being the snowiest city in America.

Allison and I engage briefly in a conversation about the Beatitudes. She does not have much of a background of biblical knowledge, but is enormously curious. Until recent years, I would have said exactly the same thing about myself. I am learning slowly.

She said, "I've been thinking about meekness. Do you think meek people get angry?"

"Of course," I answer. "I suppose the meek have just the right amount of anger at just the right time." I think that being meek, as in the bible, means not being proud. It does not mean being a victim or subservient. I have learned over the years that the concept can be tricky for women who by nature tend toward more humility, due to cultural influences. Also, some of us give our bodies to bring forth the miracle of life. That could be interpreted as being submissive, but in truth, it is much more about being creative, and participating actively in giving life. I was not exactly sure where Allison might be coming from with her question.

"Why do you ask, Allison?"

"No reason in particular," she says. "I do often get angry at the injustices done to other people."

"I think that is a very Christian response, probably exactly what Jesus meant."

"You remember how you said that another way of thinking about blessedness was to think of it as bliss."

"Yes, I do remember that."

"Well, I'm not sure that I have found my bliss yet."

"In terms of the beatitudes, I think spiritual bliss is a very high bar."

"What do you mean?" she asks.

"I certainly cannot claim that my life is marked by all eight of those principles," I confess. "I think I am making progress, and can claim some of them some of the time. If everyone could claim all of them, it would result in a new world order."

"Like the kingdom of God," Allison says.

"Yes, exactly. I believe that kingdom is about the present, or at least it begins in the present and extends into the future."

Christina and Andrea are swinging on the swings, pumping themselves. Both Allison and I look up at the same moment. From a high swing position, Andrea accidentally lets go of one side of the swing and tumbles out, her head striking the ground with a loud, sickening thump.

For the first two seconds, when our hearts stopped beating, we are frozen. Before we can move forward toward the child, Christina is kneeling beside her.

Christina gently places both her hands on both sides of her friend's head, saying, "It's okay. It's okay." Andrea suddenly jumps up, not even appearing dazed.

Allison runs to her daughter. She looks over at me, as if to confirm that we have both seen and heard the same thing.

"Andrea, does it hurt? Are you hurt?"

"No, Mommy, I'm okay."

Allison knows what I know, that a bump on the head can cause the brain to swell, and even if one thinks they are fine, they can suddenly die from a severe brain hemorrhage.

"I think I should take her to the emergency room," Allison says.

"I agree, Allison." We discuss for a few minutes whether or not we should call an ambulance, but Andrea appears so perfectly normal, that does not seem at all appropriate. Allison says that she will take her daughter to the Eastside Medical Center, where her own doctor is located. They will be able to do tests there. She insists that Christina and I need not come with her. I am so worried.

When their car pulled out of the parking space near the playground, Christina says to me, "She is all right, Momma, really."

"But how do you know Christina," I ask.

"I know," she says simply.

I believe her. Still, I am stunned by what I have witnessed, and will anxiously await a phone call from Allison. It is three hours before she calls.

"Del, she is all right," Allison tells me.

"Well, that's a miracle," I answer.

"It does sort of feel that way to me. In fact, they did a lot of tests, and could not even find any evidence of bruising anywhere. I honestly don't know how that is possible. The way her head hit the ground, I thought she might die."

"I know," I agree. I was worried too.

"I'm just so relieved," Allison says. I know that we were both going over the incident in our minds, wondering if we had seen and heard correctly, second guessing ourselves, doubting our own senses.

When we get home from the playground in the early afternoon, Christina is tired. She takes a two hour nap, without my even suggesting it. It is as if all the steam has gone out of her little sails. Maybe the fear of losing her friend had done that to her.

By the time Christina wakes up, I am able to tell her about Allison's phone called. She says nothing, but nods and smiles. She already knows.

++

I am so thankful that Eli has no meetings this evening. I need his calmness and comfort. Surely he will be able to explain away what happened at the playground.

He asks me to describe the incident to him several times. He listens with his eyes closed the second time, as if he were trying to picture it in his mind, or understand it in his heart.

We talk about the incident as if it were surely a miracle. We discuss the possibility that Andrea had not really been hurt at all. We mention the possibility of God's divine intervention.

Neither one of us mentions anything about what Christina's role might have been. I know that is because the idea is too frightening.

We make love and it is filled with awe and wonder, almost as if it is the first time we have beheld one another. That was almost four years ago now, that Christmas Eve so long ago, when Christina first came into being.

Unless, of course, she was already there in the mind of God.

CHAPTER 25

WILLARD, THE MOVIE

I have recently become curious about the making of movies, and have been researching the process on my own. Roger Riley did give me the name of the screenwriter who has written the script for the movie, *Willard*. The screenwriter is Charlotte Knight, apparently a relative of Carolyn Wilson of Ovid. From what I have learned so far, I can only assume that because they are related, Carolyn and Charlotte have some sort of financial arrangement which will be mutually beneficial. My best guess is that Carolyn agreed to take a certain percentage of the sale, when and if the project got picked up and green-lighted. It is due for release this fall.

Charlotte Knight is a professional screenwriter with quite a bit of experience. She spent a number of years working as a script doctor for a major studio, so she knows the ropes in Hollywood and in film making. I see on her website that she is represented by both an agency and an entertainment lawyer who will pursue her best interests. Knight already has several successful movie releases to her credit. From what I have been able to determine, she has been intimately involved in this project at every level.

I have no idea where Charlotte might have lived or grown up. Her bio does not provide that information. She could have some connection to New York, or maybe her branch of the family comes from Los Angeles. I do find it interesting that Knight attended the New York Film Academy in New York City and received a Master of Fine Arts. Charlotte Knight has to be one of the few really successful female screenwriters in the business. When I looked up the top ten most successful screenwriters currently working in the industry, there is not a female among them.

Through the process of researching Charlotte Knight, I discover some interesting bit of American history about which I had little prior knowledge. Charlotte Knight is the granddaughter of Dalton Trumbo, one of the screenwriters who was blacklisted in Hollywood during the time of the investigations by the House Committee on Un-American Activities. Trumbo was one of the individuals working in the Hollywood film industry, believed to be a Communist sympathizer, called to testify before the committee. The Committee's intention was to interview those believed to be planting Communist propaganda in American films. Each individual subpoenaed was also expected to provide additional names of possible Communists.

Trumbo was one of ten individuals who refused to cooperate with the House Committee and spent eleven months in a penitentiary as punishment for contempt of Congress. After being blacklisted by the Committee and writing under a pseudonym, Trumbo did eventually receive the recognition he deserved and was an Oscar winning screenwriter whose work included *Exodus* and *Spartacus.* Dalton Trumbo's son Christopher was also a television writer, a playwright, and screenwriter, making Charlotte a third generation family member to be working in the same industry. Her maiden name is Trumbo.

Learning about her story does make me hope for her sake that the movie *Willard* is successful. Still, her interest in the project is different from mine. The material came to her as a professional to write, to promote, and to sell to a production company. The film is being produced by Maple Leaf Films, a subsidiary of Paramount. I understand from what I have read and been able to find out, that Charlotte has managed to stay attached to the project through every pre-production stage, which is rare for a screenwriter. Usually, once the screenwriter has done her part, it goes into the production stage where there are multiple re-writes, which frequently do not even include the original screenwriter.

Since *Willard* is a true story, and Charlotte Knight has exclusive rights, perhaps it is not so surprising that she has managed to stay with the project as a consultant throughout filming. Suddenly finding herself in possession of a fascinating journal written by a woman from Willard must have felt like winning the lottery to Charlotte Knight. But for her, it is not personal. For me, it is deeply personal, a journal that belonged to my great-grandmother.

Since the movie will be in theaters within a matter of weeks, I am pondering whether or not I want to see it. When I decide to correspond with Ms. Knight, I hope that she might be able to answer some of my questions. She has very graciously done so.

I communicated with Charlotte Knight via email through her agency.

++

Dear Ms. Knight,

It has come to my attention that you came into possession of my great-grandmother, Deborah White's, personal journal. I am her only descendent and living relative. It was just four years ago that I discovered my own connection to Deborah White, who gave birth to my grandmother at Willard. Carolyn Wilson of Ovid, NY provided me with copies of a few pages of Deborah's journal which have to do with how Deborah felt about giving up her child. Those pages are precious to me.

Depending on how extensive the journal is, it is quite possible that you now know more about my great-grandmother than I do. I have been able to piece together some dates and locations pertinent to her life, but I do not have any personal detail, particularly from her point of view.

While I am interested in seeing the movie when it is released, I would like to ask how much of it accurately reflects her life experiences as discerned from her journal, and how much is fictional, created by those involved in the making of the movie. I do not want to come away from the film with impressions about her that are not accurate.

I have read that after a screenwriter has written a script, there may be many rewrites, according to the producer's or director's specifications. If that is the case with the movie 'Willard', I would like to know.

Any advice or insight you can give me with regard to the movie and its accuracy would be greatly appreciated.

With gratitude,
Delores Williams Fisher

I was both surprised and pleased to receive a response to my email within the week.

Dear Ms. Fisher,

What a delightful surprise to hear from you! Let me say that after spending a year working on the script, and several more working on the film, I do feel an intimate attachment to your great-grandmother, as well as her husband Dalton Duncan. I feel like I know them both personally. Ironically, my own grandfather was also named Dalton, which is not so common a name.

Yes, the journal writings are extensive and cover each decade of Deborah's life, beginning with her earliest and happiest memories. Unfortunately, there is much tragedy that follows. I do not know how much of her story you know. But it certainly is a story begging to be told because it is a story of not only survival, but also of courage and transformation, and victory over life's adversities. That is the movie's ultimate theme.

This is a once in a lifetime opportunity for a screenwriter, and I am grateful that it came into my hands. Your great-grandmother has my greatest admiration and respect. So much so that I have searched far and wide for pieces of her art work and have acquired two of her later paintings. One is of Seneca Lake scene, and the other a floral scene, lavender growing on a hillside.

One of the reasons why I have stayed so closely attached to this particular project is because I want to protect the integrity of Deborah's story. I have been fortunate to be able to stay on as a consultant, primarily because I am the owner of the material, as far as it being an original script, not based or someone else's fictional work.

There are, of course, embellishments and invented scenes throughout the movie, but in no instance are the scenes involving Deborah herself anything other than true to her own description of her experience.

In order for you to be prepared for some of those scenes, I would strongly suggest that you read the book written by Darby Penney and Peter Stastny, 'The Lives They Left Behind: Suitcases in a State Hospital Attic.' The authors spent ten years piecing together a handful of poignant biographical narratives, talking to former staff, and using artifacts from old suitcases to provide clues into some patients' lives. That book was very helpful to me.

After you see the movie, I would be very happy to hear from you and get your reaction. I know that it will be painful in many places. Yours will be a completely different perspective from anyone else's. I do hope that you will be pleased with the finished product. Also, if you wish, at some point in the future I can send to you a copy of the journal entries themselves.

I look forward to hearing from you again.

Charlotte Knight

+++

Eli and I, along with Roger and Cass went to see the movie the first weekend of September. In the opening scene, the camera moves in slowly to picture a lovely Tudor-style house on State Street in Ithaca, New York, 1916. A lovely young actress portrays a six year old Deborah White. The family sits around the kitchen table, happy and lighthearted. The bright morning sun streams in through the window, while background music is upbeat and cheerful. Gordon White is reading the *New York Times.* He comments on the progress of the war. The Americans and the French halt the German advance at the Second Battle of the Marne.

Little Deborah is coloring on a piece of paper. Susan is making scrambled eggs at the stove. It is the start of their day, as the conversation indicates. Gordon mentions an important meeting he has later in the day about his research on plant diseases.

This scene stands in stark contrast to the one that follows two years later. In September of that year, 1918, the influenza epidemic decimates the White household. The light is dim inside the house. Gray shadows fall across every room and every face. The music is dark and haunting. The flu first strikes Gordon with a dull but debilitating headache. That is followed by a burning fever.

Susan sends a letter to her sister Bernice from the city. Bernice comes to try to help, but it is already too late. After a few days, Susan also dies, leaving the young Debbie in Bernice's care. She takes the young Debbie home to Queens. Her husband, Hank has heavy features, a bright red face, drinks too much and often has mood swings. The music under this scene is scary. The movie goer can tell by the music chosen for each one of the scenes exactly what the mood will be. The ominous music surrounding the scene where we meet Hank is foreboding.

As I watch this movie, my mind is replaying the movie's shot-list that Charlotte Knight sent to me. She thought this would be helpful in preparing me for the movie. I carefully read every word of it. Each shot is numbered, along with the duration of the scene, including the cast members involved, the camera angle, and the camera movement. The first few words of dialogue are also included on the list.

While it was only a list, it does clarify for me what scenes are going to be coming up next, and who the players are. I know there are several scenes that I will not want to watch. Charlotte kindly sent me an entire packet of information from the pre-production work. So much advance planning takes place before the actual shooting begins. I am fascinated by those details.

I have learned so much about film making that I can now understand why someone would be drawn to that creative art. I have also learned that the aspiring screenwriter longs to see their creative work on the big screen in exactly the same way as an aspiring novelist once desired to see their work in print. I am sure the novelist still has that basic desire, but all media has been drastically changed and transformed due to modern technology. Many novels nowadays are only produced electronically.

Because of the shot-list, I know that the next fifteen seconds of this film will show Debbie being molested by her uncle Hank, who ended up being her guardian when Debbie's Aunt Bernice died in 1920. Deborah White is now ten years old. My heart goes out to the poor child, whose misery I cannot imagine.

This scene accounts for the lost ten years that we were never able to account for in the Deborah White narrative. She spent the next ten years, until she was eighteen, in Hank's care enduring his abuse. Both of her parents had died, as well as her aunt. Deborah writes in her journal that when she turns eighteen she will leave. We hear her thoughts as she endures her uncle's frequent visits.

Shot number twenty is the scene of her rape. The young actress who plays Deborah at eighteen is an unknown, a first time actor in a movie. I feel badly for her that this is the scene she has to endure. It is too raw and violent, and I generally do not watch such scenes. I close my eyes and think instead about the process of making a movie. I have been surprised to discover that so much of what ends up being in the movies has already been planned out in excruciating detail long before filming begins. Any notion I might have had about creative spontaneous insights happening on the set has now fallen by the wayside. A director actually has to figure out a vision before the production begins. This makes sense to me, as a detail person myself. How else could such a huge and expensive venture be managed without a detailed plan? There are storyboards, and shot lists and shooting plans and schedules. By the time filming gets underway, there are a million details already negotiated and budgeted, involving countless people and costumes, locations and props.

I know that after the scene of Deborah's rape, the next sequence of scenes take place in the Willard State Hospital. In one scene we hear and see Deborah in labor. The camera goes through a series of shots showing the faces of those in the facility who are clearly insane, or those who are deeply withdrawn. One woman imagines that she hears voices. Then unexpectedly, we hear the cry of a newborn baby, born in a hospital for the mentally ill, not your everyday occurrence. That event is dramatized by showing the reaction of those who hear the sound, wondering about its origin.

I have read the pages from Deborah's journal myself which were given to me by Carolyn Wilson about what happens next. I know how Deborah is allowed a brief period of time to hold her baby, and how she prays for her child, how she grieves and mourns, how the baby is taken from her and sent to the Foundling hospital in New York City, and from there south on the Orphan Train.

I am not surprised by the number of scenes the movie included at Willard. After all, that is the name of the movie. The latter part of the movie does show the love story of Deborah and Dalton, and how healing that is for both of them. Scenes are also included of Deborah creating her artistic work. I see a painting of lavender growing on a hillside and wonder if it is an original. It could be the same one Charlotte Knight mentioned that she owns.

An actual patient from the museum exhibit of *The Lives They Left Behind* finds his way into the story. Lawrence Marek became the institution's unpaid grave digger. I counted six different cutaways, or flashbacks in the movie, picturing Lawrence digging a grave, every time a patient died.

Lawrence was a fortunate one in some ways. He found his place and made a life, even building himself a simple wooden shack near the cemetery. He was meticulous and precise in digging his graves and found a sense of purpose for his existence. His health was excellent from his physical labor, and he continued his life's work there until his death at ninety years old.

The movie did portray some of the deplorable conditions and inhumane treatment. It did show scenes where patients received electroshock, which was the primary treatment available in the 1930's and 1940's. I would like to have seen more development of the character Dalton Duncan. They show very little of his back story. It could be that Deborah did not mention much of that in her journal. The movie did show that he was admitted to Willard in 1947. He was a soldier who had returned from World War II, suffering from post-war trauma.

My favorite parts of the movie were the scenes between Deborah and Dalton. I gained enormous insight into their relationship and how it developed. It was beautiful to see Deborah blossom and come out of her shell. The same could be said for Dalton, though he does appear less wounded than she. But he also is transformed by his love for her, which gave him the anchor he seemed to be missing.

After World War II, Magazine exposés were published depicting the awful conditions in the state hospital wards where some people were strapped to their chairs. It was due to a *Life* magazine article in 1946 that later led to the release of Deborah and Dalton. Their lives after Willard made up the last one quarter of the movie.

Following their release, Deborah created art work and made efforts to locate her daughter, to no avail. Dalton took Deborah's art to a number of different galleries. He worked at the Seneca Army Depot. They enjoyed a loving relationship for the rest of their lives.

The final scene of the movie shows both of their gravestones side by side on a hillside at the Evergreen Cemetery in Ovid. The camera moves up and away. There is a long shot and the viewer is looking down on that hillside from the sky. Then the screen fades and credits begin to roll.

++

We stop at Friendly's for ice cream on the way home and share our thoughts about the movie. I share with them my favorite parts, what I have learned that I did not already know, and some of what I learned about the process of making a movie. I watch carefully to make sure their eyes did not glaze over with boredom from my talking too much.

Cassandra asks me, "How did you like Helen Hunt as Deborah White?"

"Well, I think she does favor the photograph that I inherited, the one that was in the Everson Exhibit."

I know that Roger has brought Cass up to date on all of that. "But a photograph is flat, one-dimensional. Once the person in the picture becomes a real life actor, it is a different experience. I can relate to the woman on the screen. I think Helen Hunt is a phenomenal actress, and that was not an easy part to play. I think she was great."

"Del," Eli asks, "now that you have seen the movie, do you think Charlotte Wright will really send you a copy of the journal like she promised?"

"I believe she would if I wanted it, but you know what, I don't think I do. Now I am going to focus on the future and not the past," I answer. "I have put all the pieces of the ancestral puzzle together and now I can close that book. And thank you, Roger, for all you did to make that possible."

"Hey, think nothing of it. Thank Eli. He's the one who had to sacrifice his inheritance to pay my bill," Roger says, laughing.

Eli just smiles and winks at me.

CHAPTER 26

FOUR YEARS OLD

Christina turns four years old in just a few days. She is truly a precocious child, quick to learn, wise beyond her years, and sometimes, I must admit, a bit of a mystery to me. One of the things that I am most mystified by is the birthmark on the bottom of her foot, which appears to be clarifying. That is the best way I can describe the evolution of the mark. At birth, it was more blob-like, roughly in the shape of a plus sign, though with little definition. Over time, the outline of that plus sign has become more distinct, and I have noticed that this year, the four sides have developed a kind of bud at the ends. I hesitate to call it a cross, but I must admit that it has developed into some version of that. I do not believe that birthmarks are supposed to change, but who am I to say? Christina's is changing. At two doctor's appointments, I have asked the pediatrician, but she also seems mystified. Eli does not seem to notice the unusual mark. I rarely bring it up to him anymore.

Christina has an exceptional memory, easily able to recall anything she has seen or heard. When it is story time before bed, Eli tends to read bible stories to her. When she was two years old, he read from a child's storybook bible, with very few details for each story, accompanied by child-like pictures. When she was three years old, he used a different children's bible, one more age appropriate. This year, Eli is using *The Story Bible* by Pearl Buck. This particular version of each story is much more in depth, with greater historical detail. By this time, Christina has already heard many of the stories. She may have heard them when Eli read them to her at night. She may have heard them in her Sunday School classes at church, or she may even have heard them in worship services.

Christina has always sat attentively in church services, trained from an early age. There are other times when she is restless and needs to run around and let out her excess energy, but that does not happen during the church worship hour. I have often thought that might be because the one leading the service is her own father and she likes to hear the sound of his voice.

When Eli is reading to her, if he gets a detail wrong or omits something in a story, Christina is quick to correct him. Often I think he does that intentionally, to see if she is paying attention. Since she often has questions, I leave the bible reading activity to Eli. I focus on the more classic stories for children her age, which I get at the library every week.

Because Christina is so advanced, I have no idea how things will work for her when it is time for her to go to school. Because of her thirst for knowledge, we have been instructing her at home non-stop since she was two years old. It may well turn out that we will have to send her to some private school for the gifted. I know that the Fayetteville-Manlius schools are among the best in the state. When the time comes, perhaps she can be an out-of district tuition paying student in that district. That is sometimes allowed. We are in a position to be able to transport her ourselves, wherever we may need to take her, and also we are able to afford the cost of tuition. I am not ready just yet to look into that, because I am not yet ready for her to go to school. She herself is ready both intellectually and socially; but I am not. Knowing Eli, he no doubt has plans A through plan C already in mind for her education, but if so, he has not yet discussed those options with me.

Since Sebastian died in 2008 and Alberta two years later, we now have this huge house all to ourselves. Playing in all of the downstairs rooms is a delight to Christina. The house lends itself well to running around corners and hiding in the next room. Eli and I still occupy the same bedrooms upstairs, one for us and one for Christina, decorated largely with the color scheme and bedroom items from my previous home on Cedar Bay Road. I have done some rearranging of furniture downstairs, but I have not yet made a major decorating impact of my own. I have been well occupied these past five years, since our marriage. Often it is hard for me to fathom how much my life has changed. But the changes are all good. I have no desire whatsoever to return to my old life, before Eli, before Christina.

Before that exhibit, *The Lives They Left Behind*, I was a different person. I find it rather ironic that after encountering the exhibit of that name, my own identity could be described as having left a life behind. Thankfully, I have dealt with the pain and the truth of that, and now I feel like I have successfully moved on in a healthy way, closing out unfinished chapters.

In the past five years, besides raising a young child, I have also managed to take two courses at seminary, one in theology and one in New Testament. Since taking those courses, I have taught three different short term classes at our church. I think I have been successful in not becoming a completely traditional pastor's wife. I have observed that there are deeply ingrained ideas that people hold of what that role should be. It has been beneficial that we do not live next to the church in a church-owned pastor's home. For a person like me who had been accustomed to living alone in the woods, that would have been an especially difficult adjustment to make, giving up my privacy and solitude to live in a public place. Though infinitely larger and grander, the Fisher home in Chittenango is equally as private as my own cottage was. The house is made of brick with large cream colored columns in the front. Such a house is somewhat rare in upstate New York. Besides the two stories, there is also an attic. So far, that is a place that Christina has yet to explore. We decided to limit the access to that area for a later time when she is older.

Truthfully, even I have not explored that area of the house. Eli tells me it is probably filled with mementoes of his childhood. Someday I will explore there. Who knows what one might discover? The house has been in the family since it was owned by his great grandparents.

Roger did buy my carriage house after he and Cassandra got married. They re-modeled it to their own needs and desires. The unused space in the upstairs which I had used for storage was converted to a music room for Cass, a home office for Roger, and a work-out room for them both. A deck off of the upstairs level wraps around three sides of the house. A lovely patio beneath the deck on the back of the house overlooks the woods. A wooden circular staircase connects the upper level with the lower patio, a most unique feature.

The downstairs living area remains the same. I greatly admire all the upgrades they have done, although during the time I lived there, structural changes were not financially possible for me. Still, I would have imagined they would want a much larger house.

Roger and Cass invited us for dinner in July, after all the remodeling and landscaping were complete. We spent most of the time enjoying the outdoors, sitting on either the patio or the deck. Roger cooked steaks on the grill, and Cass made lovely dishes to accompany the meat, as well as a delicious chocolate cake, my favorite. Wine flowed freely, as well as laughter and good humor. They both seem totally happy and completely enamored with one another. I am glad for them. Neither Eli nor I thought that Roger would marry again.

++

Christina and I usually go to the Chittenango Sullivan Library for Story Time. While she listens to the stories being read, I select a pile of books for us to take home. Now she is able to read by herself at a first grade level. She has always been able to occupy herself without needing constant supervision, and now that she can read books on her own, she can read happily for long periods of time.

This Sunday, we are planning to have a birthday party for Christina in the fellowship hall after church. Many of the church folks will enjoy sharing this special time with us. I don't really have the words to describe how parishioners get attached to the pastor's family, but in some very unique and powerful ways, we become *their* family as well, and we belong to them. With her incredible memory, I have noticed that Christina can call many of them by name. I have also seen her take down the church photo directory from the phone book rack where it stays, and study the pictures. Occasionally, she will ask me a person's name, though now she can read many of them herself.

I drive to The Party House on Erie Boulevard after our trip to the library. There I buy birthday themed paper plates and napkins. I also get some streamers and balloons. I first pick up autumn colors, orange and yellow and green. Christina protests, as she is doing more often lately.

"Mommy, can't I have lavender?" she asks.

"Lavender? Are you sure you want that color for your party?"

"Yes, lavender and yellow," she says firmly.

"Those are spring colors, you know."

"If it's really my party, I should get to decide," she asserts. Chrissy is a child who knows what she wants.

"I suppose you are right about that. Okay, we'll get the colors you want," I agree. We end up getting tablecloths in yellow and lavender to match the plates and streamers.

There is a gentleman in our church named Gary Scott who knows how to make balloon animals. Those require a different kind of balloon than the usual ones you get for parties. I know if I give him a call, he will gladly make animals for the children. I will provide the type of balloons he needs.

Since we do not want the church people to buy gifts for Christina, we will simply extend the invitation during the announcement time before the service. Anyone who wishes to attend for a birthday party and cake and punch will be more than welcome to stay after the service. Certainly there will be many folks who will want to leave when the service is over, so my plan is to have the party some time following the worship service with those who remain.

Eli usually goes to the church on Saturday morning, but this week all three of us go to the church together. I need to stop at Wegman's and pick up the birthday cake I have ordered for Chrissy's party. The cake is large and heavy and I need his help.

Eli always goes to practice his sermon. To him, a sermon is a sacred offering. He says it is like the planting of seeds. One may not personally see the results of their planting, since the sprouting takes place in the human spirit. Eli always works hard on both the content and the delivery, in order to offer the best possible gift that he can. The text for tomorrow is the one where Peter asks his disciples who people are saying that he is. And then, he asks Peter who he thinks that he is. After Peter answers—the Messiah— Jesus orders him sternly not to tell anyone else. I can only assume that the time is not right for public disclosure, though Jesus wants to make sure that his disciples understand his identity. I always read the text before Sunday and look forward to hearing what Eli has to say. After having more experience now with church and more education in religion, I would describe Eli has having a rather traditional Christian theology, but delivering it with an evangelistic fervor.

Christina and I will decorate while he does his preparations. The folks who attend this church know how fortunate they are to have a pastor like Eli. The size of the congregation has grown to an attendance which is close to three hundred. The church leaders are now discussing adding an earlier service. When I asked Eli what he thought about that, he just shrugged, saying that he had led three services at his mega-church during his Seattle days. Knowing the success he had in those days, I do occasionally wonder if he will remain satisfied serving this congregation. Or will he want to seek greater opportunities?

I wonder how large a church has to be before they add additional staff. I feel that Eli is already stretched pretty thin, with all the demands of his ministry, though I have never heard him complain. The church does have a Christian Education Director, an office administrator, and a full time custodian and lots of helpers. He inspires people to want to help. Eli is an inspirational pastor.

He is always trying to identify the unique gifts of each member. He himself has many gifts, though he always seems to be blissfully unaware of his own power and magnetism. Eli has depth, knowledge, and passion, as well as charm and charisma. Admittedly, I may be somewhat biased in my assessment of my husband's abilities.

+++

I wait for more people to clear out of the fellowship hall before beginning the party. There are more people still around than I was expecting, though we have plenty of food. At my request, my helper Janet Wesley has already started filling the punch glasses for our guests. Mrs. Wesley has been Christina's Sunday School teacher for the past two years in the pre-school class.

I begin to cut pieces of the cake and place them on the lavender colored paper plates that Christina has chosen. There is a small six inch round cake set aside for Christina on which we have placed four yellow candles. There is a very large sheet cake for the congregation, as well as a variety of other selections.

Eli comes and picks Christina up, "Here's the birthday girl, let's sing happy birthday," and he starts the song as all the other guests join in. She gives her father a big hug around his neck. Shortly after the song is finished, I notice some commotion behind the table where the punch is being served. Much to my horror, I see Mrs. Wesley slump to the floor. Eli and Christina notice also. There are people all around, moving to look and see what has happened. Eli had already put Christina down, and she is almost instantly on her knees beside Janet Wesley, before anyone else even had a chance to react. She takes the short-cut by scooting underneath the table.

There are a few moments of chaos as people scramble for a cup of water, a cold cloth to put on her head. Eli removes his cell phone from his belt and immediately begins calling for an ambulance. He is well aware of Janet's struggle with diabetes, though she has always been successful in managing her disease, and no one had ever seen her pass out before. Mrs. Wesley's diabetes was diagnosed twenty five years earlier. She had been obese as a child, but lost a significant amount of weight in her twenties. At this point, she has had a lifetime of experience with the blood sugar battle and an insulin treatment for her disease management.

"Christina, come here," Eli says, urging his child to move away from Janet Wesley, who is lying on the floor. We both know that either a heart attack or a stroke are among the possibilities.

"Not yet," she answers, "not yet." With both her hands, she rubbed Mrs. Wesley's cheeks, saying, "It's all right. It's all right." Then for a brief moment, Christina lays one hand over the older woman's heart. After that, she crawls back under the table and stands beside me, as we all wait for the emergency responders to arrive on the scene. It only took three minutes. When they arrive and place Janet in the ambulance, Eli follows along in his own car to make sure that she will be all right.

Of course, everyone is frightened and concerned. I encourage them to please eat the cake. There is so much of it here. Gary Scott begins to gather the children around him making animals out of balloons. He makes some of the balloons into silly hats, and put them on the children's heads. It is good to hear the sounds of children laughing. Christina seems her normal cheerful self, unperturbed. My mind thinks about Eli and wonders how Mrs. Wesley is doing at the hospital. Eli told me before they left that they were taking her to Crouse.

After most of the people are gone, my friend Allison Wood and her daughter Andrea stay behind. Andrea and Christina giggle and bounce balloons in the air, trying to keep them from hitting the floor. Allison helps me load the car with the rest of the cake and other supplies. Quite a few people brought gifts for Christina, because they remembered that it was her birthday, or perhaps they had seen it written on some church calendar. Maybe Eli had written it on the wall calendar in the church office.

I say to Allison, "I do hope that Janet will be all right."

She seems to want to say something to me, but is hesitant. I wonder what she is thinking.

"Do you want to know what I think?" she asks, as if she has just read my mind.

"Of course," I answer.

"I am one hundred percent confident that Janet is going to be just fine," Allison says.

"What makes you so sure?" I ask, rather surprised by her certainty.

"Did you see Christina go over to her?" she asks.

"Yes, she seemed to go and comfort her," I answer.

"Yes, it did look like that," Allison admits. Then she adds, "I don't think they will find anything wrong with Janet at the hospital."

"But it could be something very serious."

"I don't think it will turn out that way," she insists.

"Why do you say, that Allison?"

"Because of what happened with Andrea," she confesses.

"You mean that day at the park?" I ask, a little afraid of what she might say.

"Yes, I heard her head hit the rock. It was a terrible sound. I was terrified. Didn't you hear it too?"

"Yes, I admit that," because I had also been terrified.

"It was Andrea who told me that Christina made her better. She said she could feel the hurt and the injury leave her body. I watched Christina under the table today. She had the same look on her face as she did at the park that day. It gave me chills both times. I don't believe it is possible that Andrea's bump could have happened without leaving a mark anywhere, without any sign of the incident, without a bruise on her body."

"What are you saying?" I ask, shocked by her statements.

"I'm saying that I believe Andrea. I think Christina made it better. And based on what I saw there on the floor with Mrs. Wesley, I think she has done the same thing again."

"I'm not sure what you are suggesting," I say, shaking inside.

"Don't worry, I won't tell anyone," Allison promises.

"No, please don't. Please don't," I beg.

I feel a chill creep up my spine.

CHAPTER 27

THE HOSPITAL VISIT

Christina and I are home by three o'clock in the afternoon. Not long after we arrive, she curls up on the couch in the den and immediately falls asleep. That is not something she usually does, but I suppose that the excitement of the party made her exhausted. We have an L-shaped couch arrangement and after I finished putting away the party supplies, I lay down to rest myself, going over in my mind everything that has happened. I want to ask Eli what he thinks about Christina, and what she may or may not have done, but I am not yet ready to do that. He knows about the incident with Andrea's miraculous recovery, but we never spoke about Christina in connection with that.

Eli arrives home around four thirty. We go into the kitchen so we will not disturb Chrissy. I put a pot of coffee on to brew. Eli looks weary.

"How is Janet?" I ask.

"They are doing lots of tests," he answers.

"And you don't know the results?"

"Her daughter Joann from Cortland finally arrived, but I don't think she had gotten any results yet either. After she arrived and we chatted, I did not feel it was my place to stay any longer. I'm sure Joann will let me know. Or I can go back to visit her tomorrow."

"Are you tired?"

"To tell you the truth, I am," Eli answers. "How is Christina? How was her party?"

"The kids had fun. But she was really tired when we got home and as soon as she lay down, she fell asleep," I answer.

"I hope she enjoyed her party despite the commotion."

"People did finally settle down after a while, and eat cake and have punch. Andrea Wood and Allison stayed around to keep us company, and the girls had fun playing together."

"I'm glad that you both have found friends in the Woods."

"Yes, we have," I affirm, trying to decide whether or not to tell Eli what Andrea said. I decide that it can wait for a while, at least.

Sunday afternoons are usually a lazy day at our house. It is a time for Eli to relax before he begins his regular routine on Monday morning. Many clergy take Mondays as their day off, but Eli prefers to take off on Friday, when he can relax because he is all prepared for Sunday by then.

Eli sits in his favorite reclining chair in the den reading the Syracuse Post Standard. There are often names that he recognizes in the paper, from the obituaries to the politicians, to the wedding announcements. His family has many connections in the area and Eli spent many years of his life in the Syracuse area as well. And of course he keeps up with the sports news for the Orange. Like most central New York natives, and Syracuse natives in particular, Eli is a Jim Boeheim fan.

We also receive the New York Times Sunday edition, which Eli enjoys reading. I often find fascinating articles to read as well. Of particular interest to me today is a review of a book called *The End of Men* by Hannah Rosin. I decide to fill Eli in on what is happening in the world, at least according to the feminist revolutionaries.

"Eli, did you know that men are losing their grip and patriarchy is crumbling?" I ask.

He responded with a nod and a quip, "Yes, that has been happening ever since I can remember."

"No, seriously, we are at the end of 200,000 years of human history and the beginning of a new era," I tease.

"The era where women rule the world, I presume," he yawns.

"Womanly skills and traits are on the rise," I quote. "Women are increasingly dominant in work and education," I continue.

I see Eli dozing off to sleep. He does not appear to be particularly interested in Hannah Rosin's world view. I go to the kitchen and begin preparations for dinner. The kitchen is a room all to itself. If I have one complaint about the house, it is that I would like to be able to see in the den while I am working in the kitchen. The idea of knocking out a wall and remodeling an entire area is more construction disruption than I can really face at the moment, or maybe ever.

++

Eli and Christina get a second wind after dinner, though tiredness catches up with me by then. Chrissy opens her birthday presents, which I faithfully hauled home for her. There are at least twenty of them. I guess there are some perks to being the preacher's kid. She delights in each gift. I write down the names of each gift giver so that I can later write a thank you note. Christina will certainly be able to sign her own name to the note cards.

++

"So what are you going to do today?" I ask Eli. We both wake up early. Chrissy is still sleeping. Eli is spreading the butter on his toasted bagel.

"I have a meeting at the church office at nine o'clock. After that, I plan to go to the hospital and check on Janet."

"I hope she is all right," I comment, thinking of my conversation with Allison.

"Me, too. If the problem was excess blood sugar, that can do a lot of damage to different parts of the body. Janet has always been very diligent in her regimen. I'll be very interested to hear what the test results show. By the time I get there, I assume that her doctor will have made the rounds and she will have an idea what they think."

"If you think of it, you might give me a call," I suggest. I could call him on his cell, but I usually hesitate to do that because he might be in pastoral situation where a cell phone ringing would be unwelcome and intrusive. I only use the cell phone if I know where he will be, or if it is an emergency. After Eli leaves for his office, I search on line and read about the possible complications of diabetes.

Christina bounces into the room wrapped in lavender streamers, laughing.

"Thank you, Mommy for my birthday party," she says." I had a good time."

"I hope it wasn't spoiled for you when the ambulance came and took Mrs. Wesley away."

"No, that's okay. She's okay," Christina assured me. I want to ask her more questions, but I am not yet ready to hear her answers, depending on what they might be.

"I got lots of presents," Christina remarks.

"Well, you are a special little four year old," I comment. "What present do you like best?"

"Hmmmm." She was thinking about that. "I like the stompers." This is the first time I have seen stompers. They look like upside down plastic cans with elastic straps on top. They are supposed to be good for the development of balance.

"And I really love the butterfly garden," she says.

"Yes, that does look like a lot of fun," I comment. She would also have been quite happy with books, but most people would not expect a four year old to be able to read.

+++

Eli did not call, as I hoped that he would. I wonder why that is the case. But after he gets home and shares with me his experiences, I can understand why he chose not to do that on the phone. I meet him at the door and ask him immediately.

"Eli, how is Janet?" I desperately want to know.

"Let's go in and sit down, Del," Eli suggests. I can tell that he looks somewhat flustered.

"Is something wrong?" I ask.

"Quite the contrary. Actually, Janet is doing exceptionally well. She told me that she had not eaten breakfast yesterday morning because her daughter called. Her daughter was having some marital problems, so Janet wanted to listen. Before she knew it, it was time to leave for church and she forgot to eat properly."

"So she passed out from low blood sugar?"

"Yes, that and also, she had been having problems with her heart, which has been blocked. She was actually scheduled for an angioplasty procedure later in the week," Eli explains.

"Oh, I had no idea. She never mentioned having any heart problems," I remark.

"Her daughter told me that she did not want anyone to know that. Both because of privacy and from pride."

"So what is the prognosis?"

"She is perfectly fine," Eli says.

"Her diabetes or her heart?"

"Both, actually. Since yesterday morning, the doctors and nurses have not been able to get anything other than a normal reading on her blood sugar levels. Hers used to run rather high."

"Are they still going to do the angioplasty?" I inquire.

"No, her heart is perfect. That is a real mystery. I talked with her doctor at length, who told me about Janet's heart problems. Now they are saying at the hospital that she has the heart muscle of a twenty five year old. And actually more like a twenty five year old who runs marathons."

"This doesn't make any sense."

"No, it doesn't," Eli agrees.

"Do you have an explanation, Eli?"

"Divine intervention maybe. As a man of God, I guess I do have to believe in that," Eli says.

"What do the doctors think?"

"They are totally clueless. Janet has been in that hospital dozens of times over the years and her medical records show many different medical problems. And yet, they all seem to have vanished."

I wasn't sure this was the right time or not, but I very much wanted to broach the topic with Eli.

"I have a theory."

"About Janet?" he asks.

"Yes. Eli, did you see Christina scoot under the table and go to Mrs. Wesley a moment after she fell, before anybody else registered what was happening?"

"Yes, I did notice that." He had a puzzled look on his face clearly not ready for what I was going to suggest.

"It's not the first time," I tell him.

"What do you mean?"

"It's not the first time that Christina has made someone better. She did a similar thing with Andrea that time at the playground. Andrea should have been seriously injured, but the tests showed nothing."

Eli sits there, shaking his head, looking shocked, saying nothing.

"This cannot be. It cannot be." Both the look on his face and the sound of his voice are filled with anguish.

I understand that I cannot push this conversation any further at the moment. It is too painful for Eli. I also know that it is a conversation we will have to continue at some point.

Chapter 28

The Phone Call 2013

To say that I am stunned by the resignation of Pope Benedict XVI would be a serious understatement. Even to non-Catholics, it is shocking news since no such thing has happened in almost five hundred years, and it is completely unexpected. Of course, I immediately think of Cardinal Conti and our visit there in 2007. Since Cardinal Phillipe Conti is an expert on papal elections, he will surely know all the ins and outs of what will be coming next and be intimately involved in every aspect of the conclave. Eli and I listen to the news with great interest. Because of Sebastian's illness, Eli had not been able to make that trip with me to Rome six years ago, where I met Phillipe Domenico Crechea Conti, the man who fathered me in the summer of 1966 as a young single man in love with a young woman. Roger and I made that trip together. I had confronted the Cardinal with my birth certificate and he did not deny his paternity.

In fact, he was rather enthralled by the idea of my existence.

Roger called last night to chat about this incredible news. I know that he got the impression when we visited that Cardinal Conti aspired to someday be the Pope. We both wondered whether or not that would be true for most Cardinals, or just some. We joked that within the next few weeks, depending on how long the election might take, that I might be the daughter of the new Pope. Roger says he wonders if that would be an historical first. We both laugh and say we doubt that. During our visit, Roger had been quite moved by the Cardinal's response to me when we met him. As a non-religious person, and something of a cynic, I think Roger's own reaction surprised even him.

March 8, 2013 is a day I will never forget. It is a Friday afternoon, so Eli is also at home when the phone rings. Eli answers it. Then he holds out the phone to me and shrugs, as if he does not know exactly who was on the other end of the phone, but that it is for me. It is a woman's voice.

"Is this Delores Williams Fisher?" a heavily accented voice inquires.

"Yes, this is she," I answer.

"Would you kindly hold for a moment? You have a phone call from Cardinal Conti."

I put my hand over the phone and whisper to Eli who it is. He recognizes the name immediately, as well as the unexpectedness of the call. His eyes grow larger, and his eyebrows shoot up.

It takes about ten seconds before the Cardinal comes on the line. "Is this Delores Crechea Fisher?" I know instantly that it is indeed him. He used his mother's family name in identifying me. No one else would have called me that. I have been called Cressie Pope. Delores Ann Williams. Delores Williams Fisher. This is the first time I have been called Delores Crechea Fisher.

"Yes, Cardinal, it is a delight to hear from you," I smile, genuinely pleased.

"The delight is all mine," he responds.

"This must be a very busy time for you," I comment.

"Indeed it is, and in a few days, as you probably have heard, a new pope will be elected."

"And are you a candidate?" I boldly ask.

"I am a potential candidate, but I assure you, it is not my time," he says.

"And are you sure of that, Your Eminence?" I wonder.

"Of course, I am privy to all the political discussions. You need not use my formal title, Delores."

"What would you like me to call you?" I ask.

"Let's think about that for a moment. We do probably need to decide. The reason for my phone call is that I would like to come and visit you and your family."

I am too shocked to speak. He continues.

"I have promised to visit my dear friend Timothy Dolan of the New York Diocese in early May. Since

I will be so close by, would it be too much of an imposition for me to drive to Syracuse for a visit?"

"You drive?" I say stupidly.

He laughs. "Well, no, not me personally. But you see I have told Cardinal Dolan that I have relatives in upstate New York, which is true. He immediately offered a driver and a car for however long I might need them. The driver also has relatives in Syracuse, so he will just be dropping me off. I hope that is acceptable."

"We would be honored, thrilled," I say honestly.

"Because my Aunt Maria had so many children, I do have many cousins across America, though I have not been in touch with them for many years. How shall we describe our family connection?" he asks.

"Let me think for a moment," I hesitate. The only real concern that I have is with Christina, and how I will explain to her how we are related. "I have a daughter, you know."

"I know, and thank you for the lovely photograph. I shared it with my mother, and she was quite thrilled. I am looking forward to meeting Christina. I have a sense that she is someone special." I sent a photo of Christina to the Cardinal when she was about a year old, but have not communicated with him since that time, nor had I heard from Cardinal Conti.

"Yes, she is indeed special. And how is your mother?" I ask.

"Sadly she passed away last year," he answers.

"Oh, I am so sorry." We have both been through recent losses.

"Thank you. Delores." He pauses for a moment before continuing. "I could easily stay at some nearby hotel, if my presence will inconvenience you in any way."

"Oh, no. We have a large house and many rooms. It will be wonderful for us to have you visit." And I meant that sincerely, already thinking of where he might sleep. Sebastian and Alberta's downstairs bedroom is the obvious choice.

"It will be a very brief visit, due to my schedule demands. I would expect to arrive on Monday afternoon of the 13th and depart on Wednesday morning the 15th, if that meets with your approval."

"Of course! I understand. Are you sure that you will still not be in Conclave by then?"

"I'm sure it will not last that long. In fact, I suspect it will be accomplished within days."

"Cardinal," I begin, hesitantly.

"Yes, Delores," he answers, sensing my uncertainty.

"How shall I introduce you to my daughter Christina? She is almost five years old and very perceptive. Hopefully, she will not ask too many questions, but with Christina, you never know."

"I assume that she already has two grandfathers. What does she call them?" he asks.

"Eli's father died three years ago. He had been ill for a long time. We have called him Granddaddy Fisher to her, and that is probably how she thinks about Eli's father."

"And your adoptive father?"

"She calls him Grandpa," I explain.

"I will let you think about that, Delores, and I will follow your lead. For starters, you can just tell her that a relative from Italy is coming to visit. Maybe that will be enough information for her. I am looking forward to meeting Christina, as well as Eli," Conti says.

"I am just so thrilled to hear from you."

"Likewise Delores," the Cardinal says.

We say our farewells and I hang up the phone.

"So, the Cardinal is coming for a visit?"

"Yes, in May," I answer.

"That would mean that he must not be expecting to be elected Pope."

"He said that this is not his time. Apparently, he is in on all the political conversations that speculate about who the prime candidates might be. He doesn't think it will be him. He is actually still quite young to be Pope, I believe. He would be around sixty five now."

Eli has a truly troubled look on his face. "I don't know the protocol for hosting a Cardinal."

"This is not an official church visit. He is visiting family."

"Shall we call him Uncle Philip?" Eli asks, jokingly, Americanizing his first name.

"I'm not sure yet exactly what Christina might call him." It is a very awkward situation. If it is this awkward for me, I can only imagine how it must feel for him.

"Actually, I'm not really sure what motivates his visit. It does seem to come out of the blue," I comment.

"I have not communicated with him in the past three years."

"I guess we'll find out soon enough. I am thinking that this visit is not something we should advertise to anyone," Eli suggests.

"That is what I am thinking also, under the circumstances."

I know that in my own life there were so many secrets, and lies of omission, that I do not want to pass along that same legacy to Christina, though I cannot figure out exactly how to explain who our visitor is. I will ponder that and hold it in my heart. I wonder if we did simply say he is "Uncle Phillip" if she would ask questions.

By keeping his visit a secret, the question does enter my mind about who I am trying to protect. Clearly, the answer to that is The Cardinal. I do not want there to be any repercussions for him from our connection, nor from this visit. But I also need to remember that I am not the one to initiate this particular visit. I did that in 2007, but this visit is all his idea.

Since that time, I have been open about my identity crisis. I have learned to own my history and my background. Doing so certainly makes me feel more at ease with myself and who I am. Since my discoveries in 2007, I have shared with both friends and family my amazing background. There is nothing there for me to be embarrassed about. I have sometimes shared that my biological father was a young Italian who later became a priest. The one part of the story that

I have kept mostly to myself, for his sake, is that that young priest is currently a member of the College of Cardinals, a professor of theology in Rome, an expert in papal elections. It has been my choice to keep that a secret. Cardinals do not generally have offspring, and to claim a cardinal as my father would feel boastful. I have no desire to boast, nor to harm his standing in any way.

Sometimes I end up holding onto secrets out of fear. Fear of the answer. Fear of the future. Fear if what it might mean to my family. Fear of the unknown, the unexplainable. At this point, there is no avoiding the unique development of the birthmark on the bottom of Christina's right foot. The ends of the plus sign have bloomed. That is the best way I know how to describe the changes. The end of each arm is split, curved back, bifurcated. I know that it is some kind of a cross. One of these days I will research crosses and see if it has any special meaning. I do not do that at the moment, because I would not know what to do with that knowledge. I do not know what kind of specialist to consult to find the answers to the questions I have about Christina.

She calls the mark her sign. "See my sign, Mommy? See how it has changed?" It is a feature that she especially enjoys and to her it does not seem in the least unusual. She does not have any preconceived notions about birthmarks. Always perceptive, Christina has picked up on my concern occasionally and has said to me, "Don't worry, Mommy, it's just my sign." I cannot say that has brought me comfort, other than the fact that it is not a concern to her.

It has been five months since Mrs. Wesley's incident at Christina's birthday party. Janet goes in monthly for tests on both her blood sugar, and every other month has an electrocardiogram for her heart. There has been no indication of any heart arrhythmia and her blood sugar level is exactly the same at every visit, and well within a low normal reading. Janet's health has not been better in years. Medical professionals are reluctant to use the words *medical miracle*, but she is clearly a mystery for them, posing unanswerable questions.

I am grateful that Janet has not talked publically about the incident as having anything to do with Christina. Perhaps she does not even know that Christina touched her. After all, she was unconscious at the time. Whenever we have discussed her improved health, she simply says, "God is good. God is so good."

CHAPTER 29

THE VISIT

The days that followed the Cardinal's phone call unfolded as he had predicted. Eli and I watched everything that was televised. Surprisingly, he is just as interested as I am. On March 12, the one hundred and fifteen cardinal-electors assemble in the Pauline Chapel and walk in procession chanting the Litany of the Saints. The presiding Cardinal reads the oath. Each cardinal elector in order of seniority places his hand on the Gospels and makes that oath in Latin. I watch in awe when Cardinal Conti comes forward to make his oath. His words are clear and strong as he speaks in Latin. It is still difficult for me to think of him as my biological father, and even more strange to imagine him visiting in our home. Even if I pinch myself, I cannot believe my connection to him, and therefore to these ancient rituals.

There are two Cardinals who are eligible to vote, but they are not present for the conclave. One from Indonesia chose not to make the trip due to deterioration of his eyesight. Another from Scotland has been accused of sexual misconduct and did not want to create a distraction and stayed away.

Too soon the Papal Master of Ceremonies called out the words "Extra omnes!"—'Everybody out!'— and the chapel doors are locked to outsiders. Once the doors are closed, the cardinals hear the second required meditation for the conclave, given by Cardinal Grech. On the first day, one ballot is taken. Black smoke coming out of the Sistine Chapel's chimney indicates that on the first ballot no candidate has received the required two-thirds of the votes cast.

The news commentators have been speculating about who might be elected. By the numbers, Europe and Italy have the majority of the cardinal electors, so a European Pope is a strong likelihood. But of course, no one can really predict the outcome. Journalists have been given unprecedented access prior to the closing of the chapel doors. The journalists say that a Latin American Pope seems unlikely, as they only have nineteen cardinal-electors. At the same time, Latin America has the largest population of Catholics.

A new Pope is elected on the fifth ballot of the second day. Jorge Mario Bergoglio of Buenos Aires, Argentina becomes the first Pope from the Americas and the first Jesuit Pope, who now calls himself Pope Francis. Even for those who have no Catholic leanings or background, the proceedings involved in electing a Pope are still fascinating.

Although Eli and I often talk about the Cardinal's upcoming visit, we have not yet mentioned it to

Christina. A five year old lives much more in the present moment, and does not look ahead months in advance the way adults do. I am still not able to refer to him, even in conversation with myself, as *my father*. I tend to think of him as *the Cardinal*, something much less personal.

The date of his visit in May is coming soon. I bought new sheets for the bed where he will sleep, the highest quality ones I could find. I have received an email from the cardinal saying how much he is looking forward to his visit in our home, and what a treat it will be to be around a young child. And of course, he is anxious to meet Christina. He says that while he is here he will not be wearing any vestments or signs of his office, and will be attired in casual clothes. That may make it easier to relate, and I will be less likely to call him *Your Eminence*. I did learn that is the proper way to address a Cardinal when I visited him in Rome six years ago.

I am greatly tempted to tell Roger Riley of the Cardinal's upcoming visit. He knows all the secrets anyway, from having thoroughly investigated my life. But Eli and I agree that we should not share this particular event with anyone, but keep it the private family gathering that it is intended to be.

We also decide that we will keep Christina at home from school on the day that our visitor is here. Because she has always been so clearly ahead of her age level in her development, we have looked into the best private school option. Eli started very early investigating educational possibilities. It was not difficult to choose the Manlius Pebble Hill School. They were willing to test her abilities and place her accordingly. When those results were evaluated, the school agreed that she should enroll early in kindergarten. She began kindergarten in September of last year, having just turned four. The MPH kindergarten is geared toward the whole child, and each child's individual needs— social, emotional, physical and cognitive. We have been quite pleased with the range of activities she has enjoyed. The Lower School as it is called, or the early grades, often brings performers and guest speakers to the campus. There are also numerous educational field trips, several of which I have accompanied as a parent chaperone.

++

I have been a nervous wreck all day today while we wait for the Cardinal's arrival. Christina knows that we are having a visitor, a relative from Italy, who will spend a couple of nights with us. We showed her Italy on the globe, half a world away. She is excited to have a guest. I assure her that he speaks perfect English. She did ask about that.

Eli has stayed out of sight for most of the day, reading in his study. Christina often goes running in to talk to him. "Daddy, Daddy, look what I found," as she holds out a daffodil flower she has picked from the yard, or "Daddy, Daddy, look what I did," as she holds out a picture she has drawn with colorful markers. Eli is never bothered in any way by her interruptions.

He is a wonderful father, patient, involved, a good listener. I do know that he worries about her sometimes. He seems occasionally concerned about her precociousness and her perceptiveness. We both just try to enjoy the innocence of her childhood. It is so exciting to see the world through a child's eyes, something I have not experienced so intimately before.

Eli told me that he had once asked Christina about the incident with Janet Wesley. She confessed to him that something had happened to her, too, but she did not seem to understand it.

"Christina, could you tell me about that time when Mrs. Wesley fell on the floor?" he asked.

"Yes, Daddy," she said.

"Did you do anything?" Eli asked.

"I'm not sure, but I did feel something," she told him.

"What did you feel?" he asked.

"I felt something come out of me," she told her father.

"And what did it feel like?"

"It was tingly and sort of hot," she answered, adding. "And afterwards, I was very tired."

"I see," Eli said.

When Eli told me about that conversation, I could tell that he knew something strange was going on with Christina, though he does not believe that she is consciously aware of anything unusual. He admits that perhaps she has some special gift.

+

At five o'clock, I notice the sedan pull into the driveway. I open the front door of the house. I cannot wait for the doorbell to ring. The Cardinal gets out of the car, and the driver removes his small overnight bag from the trunk of the car. The Cardinal exchanges a few words with the driver, who then waves as he pulls through the circular driveway.

He steps up onto the front porch to greet me. I stretch my hand out for a handshake, which he ignores and goes for an embrace. We step into the foyer of the house. Hearing the sounds of voices, both Eli and Christina arrive in the foyer at the same time, from different directions. I step back to make the introductions. What happens next is beyond explanation, other than to say it is a moment, a moment of significance, a moment that we are all caught up in. A most memorable moment.

When the Cardinal sees Christina, and she sees him, they hold one another's eyes for maybe ten seconds, not moving. Perhaps there is some special spark of recognition. I know that Eli and I both are also suspended in that moment, unable to move. Then I came out of my momentary trance.

"Christina, this is Father Conti." It just rolls out of my mouth naturally, without premeditation. I never made a conscious decision about what I might say. They both smile at one another. She looks from him to me and back again.

"You look just like my Mommy," she announces. "I think I'll call you Papa."

And that was that. It is Christina who decides how he will be addressed. I can see the twinkle in his eye and know just what he is thinking. We both know that *papa* is the Latin for Pope.

Eli comes forward. Conti introduces himself, offering his hand.

"Please call me by my American name, Philip," he suggests.

"Are you sure?" Eli asks.

"Yes, that would please me so much," he responds. "And Del, since Christina has chosen it, if you are comfortable with it, you may call me Papa, too."

I laugh out loud, out of both nervousness and relief. "I can try to do that." I know that I will never call him *the cardinal* again, though it might take a while to get comfortable with *Papa*.

Eli invites Philip into the living room. "We are so very glad to have you in our home."

"This is an impressive home, Eli," Philip says. The house is large and sits on ten acres, back off the road, though visible. There is a semi-circular driveway in front.

"Yes, it has been in my family for several generations," Eli explains.

"Del, the house reminds me somewhat of homes I remember seeing when I was in Mississippi in 1966," Philip comments.

"Because of the pillars, probably," I comment. Our home is a dark red brick two story house. The trim and the pillars are a cream color, and the four pillars run from the ground level to the second floor roof line, which make them more prominent. All the windows on the front of the house have dark green shutters. One might associate our house with a smaller version of a modified antebellum home, though it is certainly far more modest than homes from that era.

"I understand that you have lost both of your parents in recent years," Philip mentions to Eli. "I lost my own mother just last year. She was a grand lady of eighty eight."

"I'm four," Christina pipes in.

The Cardinal looks down at her and smiles. "And a lovely little four year old young lady you are! You may come and sit in my lap if you wish," he invites. She skips happily across the room and does just that. He looks distinguished, but is not the least bit intimidating in his street clothes.

Christina sits happily in Papa's lap while we have a lengthy discussion about the Pope's election. Philip seems pleased with Pope Francis, saying that he will be good for the church. He also says that just after the papal election is a good time for him to travel. He can be sure that there will be no papal election responsibilities any time soon, and he has also recently finished the semester with his students in Rome.

Eli asks, "Are you concerned about making this trip, about anyone questioning it, or recognizing you?"

Philip answers with a chuckle. "Actually, it is only during the time of a Conclave when Cardinals are celebrities. The rest of the time we can be essentially anonymous. There were no reporters waiting for me to arrive at the airport."

Eli asks him to share with us about his life as a Cardinal, and what that is like.

We have a lengthy conversation about that. Chrissy lays her head on his shoulder.

"And where exactly do you live, relative to the Vatican?" I inquire.

"Since I spend a great deal of time with my teaching responsibilities, I have an apartment at the University of Rome. It is within walking distance of the university. I also have an office at the Vatican, where I spend a great deal of time."

"What do you do there?" Eli inquires.

"I study many of the ancient and sacred documents. I am a historian, among other things," Philip says.

"Have you always been an academic?" I wonder.

"I was the Archbishop of the Diocese of Avellino in the Province of Benevito for fifteen years. But even during those years I was working on my Doctorate in Canon Law, so in a way, I have always been academically inclined."

"Can you tell us a little bit about the Vatican?" Eli asks.

"There is so much to tell. How would I choose? Do you know much about the Vatican?"

I answer, "I know very little."

Eli says, "I once saw a National Geographic special on life inside the Vatican, but I do not remember very much about it."

"Well, as you may already know, the Vatican is a sovereign nation. That was arranged through a treaty with Rome in 1929. Other than in St. Peter's Square, the Vatican is not open to the public. But inside, it is like any other nation or state or city. It has its own postal service, printing office, police force, newspaper," he explains.

I confess, "I had no idea."

"I think that besides my own work with sacred documents and historical documents, I am most interested in the incredible collection of art that resides there. Art is everywhere. Frescos line the walls and the ceilings. There are priceless sculptures, and paintings and tapestries. All of those precious works have a supporting staff that is constantly in the business of restoration. Not long ago, I looked in on a room where a tapestry was being restored. I discovered that in the process of restoring a tapestry, the artisans have access to six thousand different shades of thread," Philip explains.

Perhaps the most fascinating thing we learn about from Philip is his description of his ordination, which is clearly one of the most sacred rituals carried out by the Church.

Eli and I have both seen in film or video instances of priests being ordained when they lay prostrate on the floor. Philip says that when one is being ordained in St. Peter's Basilica, they are prostrating themselves above the bones of St. Peter himself.

Philip then tells us about an excavation which took place in the 1930's where an ancient Roman grave was uncovered directly beneath the altar. Peter was martyred and buried on a hillside outside of

Rome. Over time, that site became a shrine. It was Constantine the Great who insisted that the altar of a church be built precisely over that spot. Through research and investigation, it was confirmed in 1968 that the bones do indeed belong to St. Peter.

It is fascinating to hear Philip talk about his work and the history of the Vatican. During the day he spent with us, we show him Green Lakes State Park, on the way to Eli's church, our church. That gives us the opportunity to tell him about how Christina's made her entrance into this world. He is amazed by that, making an interesting remark.

"A humble birth indeed."

+++

I am nervous about cooking dinner, but Philip has assured me in our correspondence that he has no food issues and will be happy with whatever I put in front of him. I decide that if I stick with something quite traditional, I will be safe. I talked to the butcher personally, asking him for his very best filet mignons, and he has given me beautiful ones. The steaks, along with baked potatoes, green beans, salad, and home-made rolls have been a big hit, along with apple pie and ice cream. I explain to Philip that many varieties of apples grow in this part of New York State.

After dessert, Christina runs off to put on her nightgown. We have an opportunity for adult conversation, although whenever she is present she was always polite and rarely interrupted. Still, she is four years old and her attention span is limited.

Philip asks Eli about his ministry, and he seems genuinely interested in hearing about Eli's experiences. He asks Eli about his ordination, and it was delightful for me to hear that story again as well. He also asks about Eli's journey into the ministry, and how that had come about. Eli talks about his calling, and how it was unusual, or at least different from others he had met, since his parents were not active church participants. Eli has relied on a number of mentors throughout his ministry.

Philip says that he had known his calling from an early age, because his mother had told him that he was born to be a priest. He says that it sometimes happens in Catholic families, that a certain son will be offered up to the church. If a mother feels that is her son's calling, she will raise him for eventual priesthood. He acknowledges that in the Catholic Church, a priest's calling may very well come from his mother, or least that had been the case with him. Then he tells us that his mother, Sophia, lived her entire life as a devout Catholic by following the spiritual messages that guided her.

"You know, it's ironic. My mother always told me that I was born to be a priest. After I became a priest, she then told me that I was destined to be the Pope. I'm not entirely sure that I believe that, although I do try to stay open to that possibility. I respect the process of electing a Pope, and would neither seek it nor refuse it. Despite my mother's ambitions for me, she did have one regret."

"And what was that?" Eli asks.

He smiles, "That I would not have any children."

I add, "Yes, that is ironic."

I think this might be a good time to give him the special gift I made for him.

"Speaking of my birth, I have something that I would like to give to you, Papa," I say. I like the sound of that. Even Eli does not know what I had planned nor what this gift is. He looks at me curiously.

When I return to the dining room, I hand Philip a wrapped gift, which he opens slowly. Inside there is a lovely silver frame. He turns it over to see the other side, and inside that frame there is a picture of Iris Pope at sixteen years old, a year or two before he had met her. The look on his face is priceless. It is a mixture of both joy and pain. Tears spring instantly into his eyes. I am sure the photograph triggers many memories.

"Oh, my," he says, overcome with emotion, staring at the picture.

"In 2008, we made a trip to my grandmother's home town. I met some interesting people, including an older woman who had known my mother as a teenager. She gave me this picture. I was so happy because I had never seen a picture of her before. I thought you might like to have a copy," I explain.

"Oh, yes, thank you," he says. "She is the only woman I ever loved."

I add, to lighten the mood, "You mean besides your mother."

He chuckles. "Perhaps I should have said that Iris is the only woman I ever loved as a man loves a woman." Then he adds, "Speaking of my mother, she was delighted to learn that I did indeed father a child. And she was even more thrilled to learn that I have a grandchild."

"She must have been a very special person," I comment.

"Yes, that is certainly true." He pauses for a moment, adding, "You must wonder what precipitated this visit."

"Yes, I have wondered that," I confess.

"It is because of my mother. She actually sent me. Before she died last year, she said that I must come and visit Christina, that it was a matter of great urgency."

"Well, that is strange," I say.

"Yes, I thought so, too. When I asked her about it, she would say nothing else except—'You will know what to do.' As of this particular moment, I must confess, I still do not understand what she had in mind, but I am fulfilling my promise to her."

Eli says, "We are grateful for that, Philip." He too is mystified by this news.

"Oh, by the way, I do not want to forget," Philip says. "I brought you a gift from the Vatican." He reaches into his inside pocket and brings out a small white cardboard box.

He hands the box to me and I open it. Inside is a beautiful beaded rosary.

"I realize that you are not Catholic and will not use this in the same way that a Catholic would, but I do want you to have something to remember me by. This is one of the crosses that the Pope gives to visiting dignitaries. I asked Pope Francis if I might bring one to a very special relative. He agreed and blessed this particular rosary. I just hope that it will somehow bring you some comfort and peace."

"Oh, thank you so much, Philip, that is very kind of you. We will treasure it always," I say with genuine appreciation.

++

About that time, Christina comes bouncing into the room in her nightgown. Eli says, "I guess it is time for a bedtime story."

Christina asks, "Can Papa do it?" We all look at one another, and Philip nods happily. Soon the two of them were up the stairs to do the bedtime ritual. He must have read several stories, because Philip is gone longer than we expect. Not long after he returns to the living room, Philip says that he is tired from the traveling and would like to retire for the evening. Eli and I are disappointed, as it is early, but of course, we understand.

When we are in bed in our own room, we recall all the events of the day. We both are relieved to have found a way to address this man who is my father. I actually forgot that five years ago, Roger Riley's reaction had been just the same as Christina's—that I bear a strong facial resemblance to the man who begot me.

Later in the evening, when we are alone in our bedroom, Eli has a need to be close. He holds me in a tight embrace. I put my head on his chest. His heart beats in my ear, and soon I fall asleep to the rhythm of it.

++

Philip is up and fully dressed and has made a pot of coffee before we get to the kitchen in the morning. I marvel that he did that, but it is a simple machine to use, so probably anyone would be able to figure it out.

"I hope you had a good night's rest," I say.

"It took a while, but once I went to sleep, I did get a good rest."

"Do you have difficulty sleeping in strange places?" Eli asks.

"No, it was something else," he confesses.

"Oh?" I ask, hearing some note of concern in his voice.

"There is something that I need to ask you."

"Anything," I answer.

"Last night when Christina was in her nightgown, I could not help but notice the bottom of her foot. Tell me about that," Philip says.

"Yes," I answer, relieved to talk about it. "It started as a birth mark, but has evolved over time. At first, it was not very well defined, just a plus sign type mark. But in the past year or so, it has taken on a more precise shape. There are those split ends now, on each arm of the cross."

"Del, now I know why my mother sent me," Philip says.

"What in the world do you mean?" I ask, completely taken back.

"I did not mention this last night, because before I put Christina to bed and saw her birthmark, I did not understand the relevance myself. But my mother wanted me to bring a special gift to Christina."

"A gift?" Eli asks.

"Yes," and Philip reaches inside his other jacket pocket and brings out a small gold cross and places it on the kitchen table. It is an exact replica of the cross that is imprinted on the bottom of Christina's foot.

Eli and I are both too stunned to speak for a long time. We stare at the shiny gold object, trying to understand this moment, this connection. Philip finally speaks.

"It is a Moline cross. My mother showed me this cross when I was ordained and told me the family legend how someday the Moline Cross would find its rightful owner. Before she died, she insisted that I come and personally meet Christina. That was when she gave me the cross and told me to bring it with me," Philip says.

"I don't understand," Eli says.

"I'm not entirely sure I understand either, Eli," Philip admits.

"What is a Moline cross; what does it mean?" I want to know.

"I can tell you some things about your first question; I cannot be entirely sure about your second."

"Okay, start with what a Moline cross is," I suggest.

"It is an ancient symbol, identifiable because the ends of the arms curve back on themselves. Some have associated it with a mill. The term Moline comes from the Latin word for mill. Also, the shape of the cross is similar to the iron bar that supports a millstone. But for Christians, it is more often seen as a nautical image, like an anchor. An anchor saves. It prevents a ship from crashing. In the Christian sense, that might be understood to be about saving spiritual lives. But some have also seen it as a kind of fish hook, pointing toward the Christian responsibility to be fishers of men."

Eli and I look at one another and we both chuckle. Philip looks surprised by our laughter.

"We are the Fishers," I explain. He nods and smiles, looking pensive, remembering something from long ago.

"Now you know how I must have felt when I first learned that Iris's last name was Pope."

"I can imagine," Eli says. "But it still does not necessarily make sense. I cannot put the pieces together."

"I can only assume that my mother knows something that we do not know," Philip suggests. "When she gave me this Moline cross, she told me that it has been in her family for many generations. It is a family heirloom and treasure. It is quite valuable since it is pure gold. I have been told that the cross is well over one thousand years old, though the exact date of its origin is unknown. But I think the real value here is the family mythology. My mother said that the family myth, or prophecy, is that someday this cross will find its rightful owner. No one ever knew what that meant, but the family story kept getting passed down. Considering that Christina's mark is an exact Moline, I can safely assume that this cross belongs to her."

Eli asks, "Why would it not belong to you, a Cardinal?"

"I asked my mother about that and she said that she never had any sense that I should be the one to receive it. She kept it right up until the time of her death last year, at eighty eight years old. When she gave it to me, she insisted that I bring it with me on this trip. Now I understand why."

Eli was silent, staring at the gold cross on the table, as if it were molten lava. It is about three inches on each side, easily held in an adult's hand. I pick it up and feel it. It is heavy for its size and smooth with no rough edges, as if it has been worn smooth with handling over time.

"What are we supposed to do?" I ask.

"I cannot answer that question for you. But I do know what *I* am supposed to do, and that is to give Christina a blessing," Philip says.

"What does that involve?" Eli asks.

"Nothing more than a simple anointing," Papa answers. "That and a prayer."

"Eli, should we tell Philip about the other things?" I ask.

"Yes, I think we should," Eli agrees.

Then we tell him everything that has happened involving Christina. He listens calmly. He does not seem upset in any way, or even surprised. The calm way in which he receives this news is reassuring to us as parents. It is a relief for us to be able to tell someone. Philip affirms what we have already determined, that likely Christina has the spiritual gift of healing. He assures us that the gift of healing is a wonderful gift to have, but does agree that it is not something we would want to broadcast, in order to protect her. Even Papa seems in awe of his granddaughter's gift. I have not yet called him by the affectionate term, but I have begun to think of him as Papa.

Papa suggests that Christina is too young now to be told the story of the cross, and that we should save it until she is older before we tell her the story of her great grandmother sending it to her, and her grandfather bringing it. After spending so much time in the past few years learning about my own grandmother and great-grandmother, I suddenly wish I could have known Sophia Crechea, Christina's great-grandmother from Italy.

The blessing takes place about an hour before it was time for Philip to leave. He thought the den would be a good place. We ask if there is anything he would like for us to do. He instructs us to simply keep our hearts and minds open.

First, Papa asks Christina's permission. "Christina, would it be all right if I give you a blessing?" he asks.

She certainly understands what a blessing is, although she has never before directly been asked to receive one.

"Yes, please," she answers simply.

Philip takes a small round container out of his pocket. The container is about the size of a half dollar. It seems to be made of mother of pearl, or some other precious material, perhaps marble. He opens it and tells the three of us that this is his anointing oil. He says that it has been used in many sacred worship services, and is filled with the prayers of the faithful. I notice that its makeup is not liquid, but more solid, like a pot of gloss.

"Come, child," Philip says.

Wide-eyed, she walks toward him. He knelt on one knee. Then he begins to speak in Latin, words I did not understand. Presumably, he was reciting ancient prayers. Soon he changes his prayers to English. "Bless, O Lord, this little child, Your very own. Bless her to do Your work and Your will. Protect her. Keep her safe from harm. Guide her. Bless these parents that they may steadily guide her along the path You have chosen."

Now he is neither Philip nor Papa, but a priest, a holy man of God, carrying out a sacred and ancient rite. He places his index finger in the ointment and reaches and touches her small forehead. There he makes the sign of a cross. Then surprising her parents, Christina says words that neither of us remotely understands. I have no idea whether they were Latin words or something else. But I do believe that the holy father in our den knows exactly what she said.

"Child, your Heavenly Father has given you a double portion. May it always be used for good."

"Yes, Papa."

"In the name of the Father, the Son, and the Holy Spirit. Amen." He makes the sign of the cross.

No one speaks for what seems like a long time. There is a palatable euphoria in the room. It reminds me of what I felt at my grandmother's memorial site and at Christina's baptism. Christina is the first to speak, and that is almost in a whisper.

"Thank you, Papa," she says, as if she understands that she has just received a profound gift. I have a sense deep in my soul that she has other gifts yet to be discovered.

When the time comes for Papa's to leave, we all would have felt very sad, except we were still under the influence of a spiritual high. Christina asks Papa if she will ever see him again. He simply says that he hopes so.

He thanks me profusely for the photograph of Iris. I am reminded of what a key role another photograph once played in my own life. I hope that Philip Conti, also known as Dominico Crechea, will find comfort in the photograph that I have given to him. I thank him for the gift of the rosary. I have a feeling it is something which we will touch often for comfort.

Shortly after Cardinal Conti, Philip, now Papa, leaves, we put the golden Moline Cross in our safe where we keep important documents. We both agree that we will know when it is the right time to share this story with our daughter.

Chapter 30

A Sign
January 29, 2014

We now refer to the Cardinal as *Philip*, though I do often think of him as Papa, because Christina remembers him that way and speaks of him with affection. Children are incredibly perceptive and intuitive. At least that is true of Christina. She instantly made the connection between him and me, though she probably could not have articulated what those connections might mean. At least, she had not asked any questions.

Since his visit, Eli and I now often talk about Christina's possible giftedness. It helps that Philip addressed that directly and saw it in a positive light. Eli is now more open to that conversation. Before Philip's visit, he had a tendency to avoid any conversation that would suggest such a possibility. There have only been the two incidents—her friend Andrea and Mrs. Wesley. We have no way of really knowing whether or not we imagined her role in those incidents. They could have been mere co-incidences.

Such conversations bring up other issues for Eli. Just yesterday we were talking about Janet Wesley and how well she is doing. She has no more diabetes and no more heart disease and the medical professionals have no explanation for that. They would not typically use the term *miracle*, but it certainly does seem to apply in this case. She went from unconscious to cured. Her medical records before that incident and after the incident are proof, but the doctors keep looking for something that will give them insight into the reasons why. At her doctor's insistence, Janet goes to get checked every three months, and nothing has changed since her hospitalization last September. Clean bill of health.

Eli has been reflecting on his own feelings and beliefs as it relates to that incident.

"Del," he said to me, "just because I am a man of faith doesn't necessarily mean that I believe in the supernatural."

"Isn't the Bible full of supernatural events?" I ask, although I already know the answer.

"Of course it is," he says, "but . . ."

He did not finish that sentence. I know what he was thinking. I have had those same thoughts myself. Eli is a man of reason and logic, a man of science, definitely not one to understand the Bible to be a textbook about creation, but an account about a people of faith and their interaction with their God and their understanding that God is responsible for that creation.

Eli says, "The God of the Old Testament directly intervened in the lives of the people in supernatural and miraculous ways."

I add, "The God of the New Testament did the same through Jesus Christ."

Eli continues with our conversation, although we are mostly just thinking out loud, 'God worked miracles through other people as well. Both Peter and the Apostles had the ability to heal."

If indeed Christina has such an ability, that is frightening to us as parents. If it becomes known that she has such a gift, then how could we keep her out of the glare of the unyielding spotlight, with cameras and paparazzi, and the onslaught of thousands looking for miraculous cures? It certainly brings to mind all those occasions when Jesus warned: *Do not tell anyone.* Just the fact that we are asking these questions about Christina automatically connects her with him, and that is not something we have wanted to do. As a man of God and a man of faith, Eli has ambivalent feelings about all of this, which in some ways, I suppose, makes him doubt himself.

For me, there is no doubting the supernatural-ness of the changes in Christina's birthmark. I have always known that some things cannot be explained away with reason and logic and science. Some things are just other-worldly, and while I might not have been a religious person for much of my life, I have always been able to accept that there are mysteries. That may be because of my experience as a young child when my grandmother died. It is possible that I could have imagined hearing that voice. But the experience is vividly imprinted upon my mind that I do believe that it really happened to me, though I definitely do not understand its meaning.

There were sounds of gunshots and the smell of smoke. I lay curled up under the pew, terrified. My grandmother lay in a puddle of blood on the chancel area of the church. I knew the evil man had left, after he shouted his obscenities. I listened to every footstep as it headed out the front door. I heard the truck start up and squeal away. Then I felt a cool breeze blow on my face. A voice spoke to me. I understood it to be my grandmother's spirit saying, *You are Elisha.*

I have spent a great deal of time and energy trying to understand what that means for my life, if in fact it means anything at all. Eli has always thought that those words are somehow about me and my destiny. We have both wondered if I am supposed to pick up the mantle for my grandmother and have a ministry of my own. Since Christina was born, I have begun to feel that this strange message, or prophesy, or whatever it might have been, is more about her. I am merely the vessel. Sebastian's words just before he died were along the same line. He said: "Christina is your double portion."

Once again similar words have come to haunt us since the anointing ritual carried out by Philip with our daughter. He commented that she has been given a double portion. In the months that have passed since his visit, and the conversations that have taken place between us as parents, we have come to accept the strong possibility of Christina having the spiritual gift of healing. We do not know what to do about that, or how to handle it. We keep reminding one another that we just have to turn it all over to God. If it is truly a spiritual gift, then it comes from God and there is nothing we can add to it or take away from it.

++

"Hurry, Mommy," Christina says, "I don't want to be late."

Today I am going along as a chaperone on the school trip to the Everson Museum. Christina is very excited about this trip. I would not say that I have observed that my daughter has any giftedness in art, but being able to draw is something that I have heard her say she wishes she could do. We are leaving the school at 8:30 this morning. We should arrive at Everson by 9 o'clock or so, and then there will be a Children's Drawing Class with artist and teacher Anne Cofer. She will teach the children how to use a variety of materials, and help them to understand some of the elements and principles of art and design. It will be a hands-on class.

I have been saddened to hear just this week that the Everson Museum is facing a significant financial deficit. Because of that, two traveling exhibits scheduled to visit the museum this year have been cancelled. It is interesting to read that the cost of bringing famous exhibits often exceeds the revenue generated. I can imagine that the costs of operating a museum like the Everson are significant.

I have actually not been back to the Everson Museum in seven years, since that life-changing visit in 2007 when I discovered my own connection to the picture in *The Lives They Left Behind*. That seems so very long ago now. I feel like a different person, and in so many ways, I suppose I am. I do feel good about the fact that I have been able to uncover my own story, and perhaps more importantly to come to terms with it, to own it, to integrate it into my heart and soul. From Willard and Deborah White to Christina Fisher is an incredible family saga spanning five generations.

And here we are today, perhaps coming full circle in a different way, back to the museum where that journey began.

There is some lake effect snow predicted, but it does not seem to be serious enough that schools have closed. It has been a severe winter this year, with a lot of snow and weeks of below freezing weather. The sub-zero weather pattern, now being called the artic plunge, has not happened in several decades. The frigid temperatures require proper layering of clothes if one is going out, making sure you have gloves and a hat and are protected against the elements.

Christina is impatient with me, so finally we are off, making the drive to the Manlius-Pebble Hill School. The snow is coming down pretty hard. I am driving very carefully because when it is actively snowing is the most tricky time to drive. We do arrive in plenty of time and report to Mrs. Daniels class.

Christina's teacher is a warm and energetic thirty year old. There are twenty two students in her first grade class. Mrs. Daniels, her teacher's assistant, and two other parents are accompanying the group on this field trip. All of us help the children with coats and boots, if they need help. Or we make sure they have their hats and gloves. Mrs. Daniels goes through the check off list, to make sure that we all have everything we need and are prepared for our journey. The school has provided the lunches, and the museum is providing a private space for us to have our lunch. After lunch, we will see the Chinese Ceramic exhibit which is on display. Cloud Wampler donated Asian works to the Everson Museum. The collection spans nearly two thousand years of history and contains a variety of forms, styles and glazes. A ceramic demonstration is planned for the children, showing them how the clay is poured into molds.

Since there are only twenty six of us making the trip, we are traveling today in the smaller school bus. The full size bus has more room than we need. Soon we have left the school grounds and the driver, Robbie, is driving very carefully. Christina is sitting with a classmate several seats behind me, on the opposite side, and I am sitting with another parent, Lily, Adam's mother.

We have not traveled very far at all on Jamesville Road when the snow begins to intensify. One has to be careful in this kind of snow storm because sudden and unexpected white-out conditions can occur. Usually, one presses on because a tenth of a mile up the road, conditions can be completely different. At the moment, what we are facing an intense squall. I am sure that we are all wondering whether or not we should turn around and head back to the school. By the time we are passing the Butternut Creek Golf Course on our left, visibility is non-existent. Then a very strange thing happens. I hear Christina's voice speaking loudly.

I turn around and see that she is standing and her eyes are closed.

"Snow, snow, go away," she yells.

It is hard to describe what happens next. No one can really understand it or fathom it. All the snow in our range of vision, as far as we could see, gathers into a funnel cloud like a whirlwind. Immediately, it lifts itself like a white swirling tornado and rises up into the sky. Then Robbie sees another school bus which has obviously skidded into a horizontal position, directly across the road as it came off of Nottingham Road. Robbie slams on the brakes and our bus skids. It comes to a stop just inches before we slam into the other full sized bus, filled with school children.

Then all pandemonium breaks loose. There are screams from everywhere. Some of the children are crying. We have to find out if anyone is hurt, I think to myself. People are frantic.

Robbie, the bus driver, is clearly shaken. A terrible tragedy has just been averted. As many as 90 people in the two busses could potentially have been injured.

"What just happened?"

"What's going on?"

"Did you see that?"

"How could that have happened?"

"Thank God we stopped in time."

Lily and I both jump out of our seats and begin checking and comforting the children. There are some small bruises and scratches.

"Christina, are you all right?" I ask, as I pass her seat. She just nods. I have to ask her about what has happened, but that has to wait.

Robbie exits the bus to check on the other bus and its occupants. The two drivers stand and look at the two inches between the nose of our bus and the side of theirs. Since our bus is smaller, we might have gotten the worse impact, though the students seated on that side could have been badly injured if contact had been made. There are no injuries on that bus.

Mrs. Daniels checks with each child to make sure there were no major injuries. Two had fallen off of their seat when the bus had suddenly squealed to a stop, but they had not been hurt. There were no head injuries or broken bones.

The five of us adults have a conversation just outside the bus's door about what we should do next. Should we call any authorities? There was really no accident to report. Should we call the school? Mrs. Daniels said that she would call and inform them. We discuss whether or not we should continue with our plans to visit the Museum. By now the snow squall seem to have cleared away. Robbie backs our bus away from the side of the other bus. That bus, which has slid on the ice coming from Nottingham Road managed to right itself. Although everyone is clearly shaken up, and probably will be for a while, we all agree that we should continue on our trip.

Lily pulls me off to the side and whispers, "Del, do you know why Christina was yelling right before we nearly collided?"

"Maybe she was afraid of the snow," I suggest, having no idea what to say.

"Am I imagining what happened, or did the snow disappear after she yelled?"

"I think maybe those two things were not too far apart," I confess.

Lily seems confused and amazed and needing some kind of an explanation. I am not able to give her that. I need to know myself. When I get a chance, maybe when we get home, I will ask Christina about it myself. I am just as shaken as everyone else. But how fortunate we are that no one on either bus is seriously injured. Both vehicles have been able to right themselves on the road and continue on their way.

The snowfall is very light now, as we drive slowly along Rt. 481 South, before we pick up Rt. 81 North, which would take us to the Harrison Street exit and the museum. By the time we get there and pull into the school bus parking area, the children have calmed down, though they are still excited.

Our tour guide meets us and takes us first to the art room where the children with meet with the visiting artist, Anne Cofer. Depending on their interests, the children can choose watercolors, or charcoal pencils, or even acrylic paints for their creations. Ms. Cofer is a patient teacher, offering positive encouragement to each child. By lunch time, the children are back to themselves, laughing and talking excitedly, the earlier incident almost forgotten.

Over the course of the day, I feel several times that Mrs. Daniels wants to speak to me, but held back. If she asks me any specific questions about Christina's yelling incident earlier in the day, I do not know how I will answer her. But that did not happen. We all return to the school around 2:30 that afternoon.

As soon as we are in the car, and Christina is buckled into her booster seat, she falls asleep. I drive home, desperately wanting to talk to Eli. He is usually home by 4:30 in the afternoon. Sometimes he has to go back out in the evening for a meeting or a counseling session. I can only hope that is not the case today.

Christina is still sound asleep when I pull into the garage. I am surprised to see that Eli's car is already there. I go in the side door, which leads into the mud room between the garage and the kitchen.

"Hi, Del, how was your day?" he asks, before he has really looked carefully at my face.

"Eli, Christina is asleep in the car. Would you bring her in and take her up to her room for a nap?" I request.

Eli can immediately tell that something unusual has happened. Christina rarely naps in the afternoon. But now she is out cold, and did not even wake up when her father carried her from the car up the stairs. Then he joins me in the kitchen. We sit down at the kitchen table.

"Del, what's wrong?" Eli is keenly aware of how frightened I look.

"There was an incident this morning with the school bus," I say.

"Is everyone all right?"

"Yes, no one was hurt, but it was a very close call. We were in the middle of a squall and almost broadsided another full size bus full of people. It was turned cross ways in the road."

"Oh, Wow! That must have been scary," Eli comforts. "Was Christina frightened?"

"Well, I can't say exactly."

"What do you mean? You were there."

"There was a strange incident." I say softly.

"Involving Christina?"

"Yes."

"Maybe you'd better tell me about it."

"I will do the best I can," I respond, taking a deep sigh and letting it out. "Eli, we were in the middle of a blinding white-out and for a few seconds there was zero visibility. That's when Christina yelled."

"What do you mean she yelled?"

"I happened to turn around when I first heard her voice. She stood up, grabbed on to the back of the seat in front of her and closed her eyes." I paused for a moment, feeling shiver crawl up my back. "I am pretty sure that she cried out 'Snow, snow, go away."

"Was it a childish song, like 'Rain, rain, go away?"

"I suppose it could have been. She might have been singing a child's song. Except for what happened next."

"What happened, Del?"

"The snow stopped. No, that's not quite right. The snow all went into a cyclone shape, like a tornado and lifted up into the sky like a whirlwind. Immediately the other bus came into view and our driver, Robbie slammed on the brakes. We slid close to the other bus and then came to a stop just inches from its side."

I cannot read the look on Eli's face.

"My God," he says. We sit together there for several minutes and neither of us speaks.

"Del, could you please describe how her voice sounded when she yelled?"

"It certainly was not the sound of playfulness. It was more like a command," I answer.

"You mean to tell me that she commanded the snow?" Eli asks.

"I think so," I answer.

"What did the other people say?" Eli asks.

"There was some mumbling going on, and Lily, Adam's mother asked me whether or not Christina's yelling had anything to do with the snow disappearing, so she must have made some connection, or had some thought."

"What about Mrs. Daniels?"

"Well, after everyone calmed down and we established that no one was hurt, we all decided to continue with our field trip to the museum. Several times during the day, I thought that Mrs. Daniels was going to say something to me, but she never did."

"Have you talked to Christina about it?" he asks.

"I would have, but she fell asleep as soon as we were in the car on the way home," I explain.

"I see," Eli says.

I wonder what he sees. He seems to read my mind.

"Using her gift drains her. She is always exhausted afterward," he says.

I pause for a moment to recall the other two incidents, and he is right. On both of those occasions, where we suspect there was a kind of miraculous healing, she had been very tired.

"Eli, I don't really understand any of this," I confess.

"I know," he answers. "I don't think these are the kind of events that can be explained with rational explanations."

"But you have a theory?"

"Well, I did before today," Eli says. "Before today, I had accepted that our daughter likely has a spiritual gift of healing. But I have honestly never heard of a child so young using such gifts. I wasn't even aware such a thing could happen. From what I have read about these things, that kind of spiritual gift would not manifest itself until adulthood."

"So what makes today different in your mind?"

"Today's incident was not about healing," he answers somberly.

"You are right," I realize.

Suddenly Christina appears at the doorway to the kitchen. She is such a young child. Now she is dragging her favorite blanket.

"Are you talking about me?" she asks.

"Come give your Daddy a hug," Eli says. "I haven't seen you all day. Did you enjoy the museum?"

"Yes, but I was tired," she says.

"Why were you tired, honey?"

"It was because of the snow," she answers.

"Tell me about that, Christina," he urges.

"Okay. There was a lot of snow. I knew the driver could not see the other school bus, but I knew it was there," she says.

"How did you know Chrissy?" I ask.

"I just saw it in my mind," she explains.

"And then what happened?" Eli asks.

"Then I knew I had to help," she says. "Somebody could have gotten hurt."

"I'm glad you wanted to help, Christina," Eli says. "Tell me what you did next."

"I know I asked for help, and then I cried out," she says.

"You asked God for help?"

"Yes."

"And did God help?" Eli asks.

"God took away the snow just in time," Christina says.

"Can you tell me anything else about that?" Eli asks.

"It went away in a whirlwind," Christina describes.

"Like a tornado?" Eli says.

"Yes."

"Were you afraid," I inquire. She is, after all, not yet six years old, a very young child.

"No. I commanded it. And it stopped."

Neither one of us knows what to say to that. We are silent for a moment.

"And how do you feel about that, Christina?" Eli asks.

"Well, I hope I don't have to do it again anytime soon. It makes me tired. I think I'm too little for such a big job."

"I think so too," I agree emphatically.

Eli says, "Maybe we could ask God not to give you such big jobs until you are a little older."

"I don't think that will work, Daddy," she says.

"You don't? Why not?"

"Because I'm supposed to help. That's my job."

"Christina, you are too young to have a job," Eli insists.

"Too young to help?" she asks incredulous.

"No, just too young to do miracles," Eli says. "You must wait until you are older and it won't make you so tired."

"Okay, Daddy" she says with uncertainty. "I'll try not to."

+

I think of the double portion that has been allotted to her and wonder what it will mean.

++

How does one parent such a child? How do we protect her, I wonder? What will happen to her when she is older? Or if people find out? Even as I ask these questions, I know deep in my heart that whatever God has called into being will work according to God's purposes, in God's time. It does not belong to us as her parents either to claim or to limit. All that we can do is try to protect her, and stand in awe and wonder before this sacred power, whatever it is.

All that we can do is pray that she will be able to bear the portion she has been given. God help us.